WITCH
Family Values Prequel
Book 0

Patrick Logan

Books by Patrick Logan

Insatiable Series
Book 1: Skin
Book 2: Crackers
Book 3: Flesh
Book 4: Parasite
Book 4.5: Knuckles
Book 5: Stitches

The Haunted Series
Book 1: Shallow Graves
Book 2: The Seventh Ward
Book 3: Seaforth Prison
Book 4: Scarsdale Crematorium
Book 5: Sacred Heart Orphanage
Book 6: Shores of the Marrow
Book 7: Sacrifice

Family Values Trilogy
Witch (Prequel)
Mother
Father
Daughter (Coming Soon)

This book is a work of fiction. Names, characters, places, and incidents in this book are either entirely imaginary or are used fictitiously. Any resemblance to actual people, living or dead, or of places, events, or locales is entirely coincidental.

Copyright © Patrick Logan 2016
Cover design: Ebook Launch (www.ebooklaunch.com)
Interior design: © Patrick Logan 2016
Editing: Main Line Editing (www.mainlineediting.com)
All rights reserved.

This book, or parts thereof, cannot be reproduced, scanned, or disseminated in any print or electronic form.

First Edition: October 2019

Prologue

The old croon's eyes didn't work, hadn't worked in some time, in fact, but she never stumbled. The wooden cane gripped between her gnarled fingers helped, but it wasn't necessary.

The woman didn't need to see. She didn't need to smell either, but she was keenly aware of the stench of rotting vegetation that clung to her rags.

She had been moving through the trees, leaving bare footprints in the mud, for as long as the swamp had existed.

She'd been there when the blood of Askergan sacrifices had tinged the swamp red. She'd been there when the Tuscarora war had broken out, and she'd been there when it had ended.

The croon had been there before and she would be there after.

Although she moved in and out of the trees without abandon, she was rarely spotted.

Nobody wanted to see her crooked spine, her thinning gray hair, least of all her disturbing white eyes.

But every twenty years, she had to come back.

Every twenty years, she kept things in check.

The woman drove the tip of her cane into a section of brown bog. Bubbles rose to coat the end, frothing with anticipation. In the failing afternoon light, they looked orange, or maybe even pink, like scattered fish roe. Something was coming, and the swamp knew it. Something that was supposed to stay buried was destined to return.

The old croon blinked and turned her cataractous eyes skyward. The witch's ears weren't nearly as good as they used to be, but she could still hear the screams from the Marrow.

Part I - Stolen fruit

Chapter 1

A bullfrog croaked somewhere to Anne's left, a throaty, resonating belch, and she nearly jumped out of her skin. Her heart was already pounding away in her chest, but now it took off like a jackrabbit chased by a rabid dog.

Her breath was coming in short, tight gasps, and her entire body started to tingle.

A frog—just a croaker. Calm down, Anne. No one's here—no one has seen you yet.

Her calm, rational thoughts did nothing to calm her nerves. Feet rooted in the mud, she waited for a full minute before finally mustering the courage to move again.

Anne LaForet was not a thief. In fact, over the course of her twenty-four years, she had never committed a single crime. But that was then, and this was now. Then, she had had a husband to support her. Now, she had no choice—the survival of both her and her daughter depended on her breaking the law.

Anne knew the consequences of being caught, but she also knew the consequence of returning home empty-handed. She swallowed hard and nodded, a silent affirmation of her actions.

I have to do it. I have to.

Anne slowly lifted one of her bare feet from the mud. The thick, foul-smelling substance clung to her heel like fingers, but with a sharp yank, it released her. There was a gassy sigh as the mud backfilled the divot her small foot had left behind. Shifting the empty burlap sack to her other arm, she took another step, and then another, her confidence building the closer she got to the garden.

The moon was full this night, for which Anne was grateful. Not the most sure-footed even in daylight—the scrapes on her knees from the various falls this past week alone were proof enough of her clumsiness—she couldn't even imagine doing what she was about to do if it had been overcast.

As it turned out, tonight was perfect: the air was still and calm, and for what seemed like forever, it seemed just a smidgen cooler than it had been all summer. And then there was the moon, smiling down at her with its lipless mouth, a giant, glowing orb of a face that seemed to encourage her.

Go on, you can do this; you have *to do this.*

It took another ten steps before Anne finally made out the outline of the peaked roof of the Thomases' house that stood out against the ubiquitous background of stars. Her eyes scanned the windows, moving back and forth quickly, desperately, searching for movement, the flicker of a lamp, anything at all that would send her back to the safety of the swamp.

Nothing.

Which was good.

And bad.

Good because, as she had suspected, the Thomases weren't home—rumor had it that they traveled north to visit Veronica's cousin who was full with child. But it was also bad because now Anne had no excuse to turn back.

Think of Terry. Think of Terry waking up again in the middle of the night, crying because her tummy hurts, that she can't sleep because it kept talking to her, that it was eating itself because she was so hungry.

She could have killed Steven Merch for telling her that. And maybe the boy's parents, too, because undoubtedly the idea of a person's stomach eating itself from the inside out had come from them first. After all, neither Teresa nor Steven were even four... and what three-year-old could come up with something like that on their own?

Anne was not oblivious to the fact that others in the swamp talked about her and Teresa. She may have been poor, but she wasn't stupid, despite what they said. Sometimes Terry told her what she overheard other kids saying, or, like Steven Merch, what they said directly to her, and occasionally Anne heard these rumors firsthand. More often, though, it was what people *didn't* say—at least, not with words—that made their disdain for them so plainly obvious. It was in the way that they wouldn't look directly at Anne when she approached, or the way they stared when they thought she wasn't looking.

But Anne knew.

And it filled her with sadness.

It wasn't her fault that her husband had died. And the way he'd died... that was honorable, wasn't it? Shouldn't they have been supported by the community, rather than treated like one of the sick women with the oozing sores and the clubbed feet?

But it was just the way of the swamp; they had their beliefs ingrained, and nothing Anne said or did could ever change that.

They hated single mothers, thieves, and witches, and it would always be that way.

Anne shook her head, trying to force these thoughts away; she would have time to reminisce later. Right now, however, she had a job to do.

For her, but mostly for Terry.

The Thomases' garden was more plentiful than Anne could have ever imagined, and greed quickly usurped fear or guilt as her primary emotion. She had never seen so many ripe vegetables—everything from eggplant to pumpkin to lettuce and tomatoes, all perfectly ripe for the picking—in her entire life. Having only seen the Thomases' house, one of the bigger houses in the swamp, from the road, she had had no idea that their garden behind was so *expansive*.

With eyes like saucers, Anne reached down and plucked a tomato that was larger than her fist from the vine closest to her. Its flesh was pliable, just the perfect amount of give between thumb and forefinger. She opened her burlap sack to toss it in, but hesitated at the last second.

This time, however, it wasn't guilt that struck her, but something else, something more primal.

It was hunger.

Anne bit into the fruit and experienced something akin to an orgasm in her mouth. The sweet flesh nearly exploded between her teeth, sending seeds and juice squirting from her mouth.

It was all she could do to contain a giggle.

Wiping the mess from her chin with the back of her hand, she took another quick bite, then a third, barely chewing in between.

It was so delicious that she had to fight the urge to sit down in the mud and gorge herself until she was a huge blob, too fat to even roll away when the Thomases finally came home.

Thoughts of Terry back home pushed this silly idea from her mind, and she finished the tomato, licking her fingers clean when she was done. Then she picked two equally ripe and delicious-looking tomatoes and put them delicately into her bag. Now that she had tasted the delicious fruit, she was cautious not to bruise them. She wanted Terry to try them as she just had, to experience the pure joy that forced her heart-shaped mouth into a massive grin—so massive, in fact, that her cheeks started to ache.

Anne moved to the cucumbers next, devouring an entire seven-inch vegetable in less than five bites. It was cool, crisp, and goddammit if it wasn't the best cucumber she had ever eaten.

Two of those went into the bag with the tomatoes.

For the next twenty minutes, Anne devoured more fruits and vegetables, filling first her stomach and then the sack until it was nearly bursting at the seams—until *both* were nearly bursting.

Breathing deeply, Anne started to make her way back to the wooded swamp from where she had come. She was both less cautious and less mobile now that her tiny stomach had been filled to the brim, and it took her nearly twice as long to get out of the garden as it had taken to contemplate whether or not she should enter.

When she finally stepped over the small wooden barrier and was safely on the muddy embankment, she turned back to take a look. Her heart sank.

When she had first come up with this plan, she had promised herself to take just a handful of fruit, three, maybe four items at most. But just the sight of the riches of lush vegetables had overwhelmed her and now, looking back, she could barely swallow. Not only were there large areas of missing fruit, sometimes entire plants devoid of any produce at all, but she could also clearly make out footsteps in the mud that formed tight circles followed by long trails as if someone had been practicing some sort of ritualistic dance.

Shit.

With two or three fruits missing, the Thomases might have assumed that the raccoons were back, despite Ken Thomas's encouraging musket blasts that she could occasionally hear from her place. But the way it looked now, even if all of the raccoons in the entire swamp, and maybe a family of gators, had ravaged the garden, she doubted they could have made as much of a dent as she had.

And even if Ken Thomas were to believe this, he would also have to believe that the swamp animals had used human footprints to mask their efforts. Not even a drunk like Ken Thomas would believe that. Anne stood frozen for a minute, wondering if she should try and put some of the fruit back, to go back into the garden and mess up some of her footsteps.

No, that's stupid, just—

There was a flash of light from one of the upstairs windows.

Anne felt her heart leap from her chest into her throat. Only now she was too full to swallow it, to force it back down again.

A lantern illuminated the upstairs of the Thomases' house, and Anne spun in the mud so quickly that she nearly fell.

Putting a hand down in the warm substance to steady herself, she stood and ran as fast as her legs could carry her, only partly aware that some of the fruit and vegetables that she had collected had spilled from her bag.

In her mind, all she saw was Veronica Thomas's face in the window, looking down at her with squinted eyes.

Anne prayed that the woman was blinded by the moon or that she was hidden in the shadows when the woman had looked out. Because she knew what happened to thieves in the swamp. And Teresa was far better off hungry than alone.

Chapter 2

Anne was too scared to even open the bag the day after she had stolen the fruit, let alone eat from it. Instead, she had stashed it in a box in her closet, worried that at any moment Ken Thomas would come by and search the place. Still, as scared as she was, she was equally as hungry, and this prevented her from throwing the produce away.

She spent the entire day on the porch swing with Terry playing in the grass and mud in front of her. She told her daughter that it was a hot day and that it was best for her to spend time outside instead of cooped up in the house, but the truth was that she wanted the little girl to be there if Ken came around. After all, he wouldn't dare do anything too drastic with a three-year-old present, would he?

In the end, it didn't matter. No one came, and by evening, as she sat at the table with Terry, both of them choking down dry oats and the last of the bitter berries that Anne had found after a three-hour hike through the swamp, her eyes kept darting across the simple kitchen to the bedroom.

And her thoughts about the way the tomato had burst in her mouth, the sheer coolness of the cucumber as she bit through the crunchy exterior, and the squeaking of the slick outer skin of the eggplant, pervaded her every thought.

"Mommy?"

Anne swallowed a lump of dry oats, wincing as the wad scraped its way down her throat. Then she looked up, a smile spreading across her face despite the tasteless meal, inspired by those large blue eyes.

"Hmm?"

"Thirsty, Mommy."

Anne pointed at Terry's bowl with her wooden spoon.

"Finish your oats, then you can have some milk."

The girl's cute face transformed into something different; it contorted like a balled-up sock.

"But it's so dry," she whined.

Anne pointed more aggressively.

"Eat," she instructed. "And don't make that face. Makes you look like a dog."

Teresa responded by exaggerating the expression.

"I wish I had a doggy."

Anne sighed and scooped another mouthful of the oats.

"Me too. But this world isn't for wishes, Terry. Just eat, okay? Then you can have some milk. Besides, I should finish first... I need the energy."

The girl relaxed and nodded. Then she scarfed six or seven spoonfuls into her mouth in less than a minute.

"Done," she said, her mouth still full. The girl tilted the bowl to show Anne that she was, in fact, done.

Anne smirked, and Teresa's smile grew, showing her the gray-beige wad in her mouth that covered her tiny teeth. Anne finished her own porridge in one massive bite. Then she too smiled, revealing her own mouthful to her daughter.

"Me too," she said. The words came out like *'me thoo'* and a speck of oatmeal flew onto the table. Teresa giggled, her small hand covering her mouth to prevent the same thing from happening to her.

It was all Anne could do not to break out laughing and spew her porridge all over the place. With a thick swallow, she finally downed it all. Then she showed Teresa her bowl, as the girl had done to her moments ago. They both laughed.

"Okay, you rascal," Anne said, unbuttoning the front of her blouse. "Come sit on my lap and have some milk."

Anne rose early the next day, making a point to be up before Teresa, who often awoke before the sun even had an inkling of rising in the sky. After a quick glance into the morning dawn, and confirming that the red-faced Ken Thomas wasn't standing on her porch or peeking in through the window, she went to the closet and retrieved the bag of produce. She pulled out every item and laid them on the floor, unable to contain her excitement as she took a mental inventory.

Three tomatoes.

Two cucumbers—but big *cucumbers.*

Two eggplants.

One head of lettuce.

Six radishes.

Four carrots.

Three potatoes.

Anne's hands were shaking with excitement. It was enough food to last them a month if they rationed it properly—and if they stayed fresh in the cupboard. She was most excited about the tomatoes, her mind racing back to two nights ago when she had stood bathed in moonlight, tomato juice and seeds speckling her chin.

Still, it wasn't *that* much food, and Anne was beginning to think that perhaps she overestimated how much it would be missed from the Thomases' garden. Thinking back to that night, she considered that maybe the garden hadn't looked as barren as she had initially thought. After all, her mind had a way of playing tricks on her, and her imagination had a penchant for running wild.

At least that was what Wallace used to say.

It took considerable effort to put the food back in the bag, to not test each and every item again, to confirm that not only were they real, but that they were *amazing*.

She put all of the fruit back in the bag, save one tomato—the smallest one—and then placed the bag back in the cool cupboard.

Then she went to the kitchen and put out plates for breakfast. She plopped the entire tomato down on Terry's plate.

Taking a step back, she surveyed the scene for a good minute imagining the expression on her daughter's face when she saw the tomato.

Will she even think it's real?

Anne chuckled, then tiptoed back to bed.

"Mom." The voice was distant and indistinct, as if spoken underwater. "Mom!"

Anne rolled away from the sound, but then she felt a small hand grab her arm. Her eyes snapped open and she turned to face her daughter, who was standing over her, tears in her big blue eyes.

She sat bolt upright.

"Terry? What's wrong? Terry?" She drew her daughter into her, holding her against her chest as they both sat on the bed.

"I did something bad, Mommy, I think."

"Shhh," Anne hushed, stroking the girl's blonde hair.

Teresa's back hitched and she let out a sob.

"It's okay, sweetie. It's okay."

After the tears passed, she put a finger under the girl's chin and raised her gaze.

"What happened?"

Teresa looked away, but said nothing. Instead, she interlaced her fingers with Anne's and together they stood. Then Anne was led into the kitchen.

"Terry? Just tell me—"

Anne's eyes fell on the table and she immediately burst out laughing.

"Oh, Terry! It's alright! It's okay," she said, trying to get the words out between chuckles.

Teresa's face changed again, transitioning from sadness to anger.

"Why you laughing?"

"Oh, because, sweetie, it's *okay*."

Teresa pulled her hand away.

"Not funny," she said with a pout. "Not funny, Mommy."

Anne stared at the half-eaten tomato and the spray of seeds and juice that arced nearly all the way across the worn pine table.

"It *is* funny," she insisted. "The tomato was for you, dear. Now go eat the rest before I get to it!"

Chapter 3

Anne was still chuckling when there was a knock at the door. Her laughter ceased immediately.

"Mom?" Terry asked, a concerned look on her round face.

Anne held up a finger to silence her. She waited, thinking that maybe the person would go away—or had never been there in the first place, that she had imagined the knock.

For nearly a minute, there was nothing—only the sound of Anne's breathing.

And then it came again, three sharp raps against the door, the sound echoing throughout the wooden house.

"Anne? Anne, I know you are in there. Answer the door, Anne."

Anne stopped breathing entirely. She recognized the voice.

It was Veronica Thomas.

"Mom?" Terry asked in a small voice. Anne sucked in a fresh breath, her lungs burning as they re-inflated. Now, in addition to her gulps of air, she could also hear her heart pounding away in her ears.

"You 'kay?" Terry whispered. Her bright blue eyes, so full of joy and humor but a few minutes ago, were now filled with fear. "Mom?"

Anne couldn't respond, couldn't even move. It was as if she were back in the swamp behind the Thomases' garden again, but now when she tried to raise her feet, she couldn't. The mud was unrelenting, wet black fingers holding her heel to the warm muck.

"Anne?"

Another glance at Terry's face and Anne snapped out of her frozen state.

"Coming!" she croaked. And then she made hand gestures to Terry, indicating for her to hurry, to finish the last of the tomato. The girl obliged, swallowing what remained in one bite. "Now go to your room, okay, sweetie? Just play with your imaginary friends again, or play with one of the wooden scarecrows, if you want."

The girl still looked frightened, but she pushed back from the table nonetheless. Before she left the kitchen, she held up her plate, which was smeared with the remnants of the tomato.

"Sink, Mommy?"

Anne shook her head and hurried over to the table, taking it from her.

"Just go to your room, Terry."

She patted the girl's head to reassure her that everything was going to be okay, but it was a forced gesture, her hand moving robotically. Unlike the day prior on the lawn, she didn't think that having Terry present *inside* the house when Veronica confronted her would be a good idea.

"Anne?" Veronica asked again from behind the closed door.

"Coming! One second!"

Anne hurried to the basin and dipped the plate in the stagnant water that she had pulled from the well a few days ago. The water was dirty, and the tomato seeds seemed to float to the top for a second. In her mind, they were the most obvious things in the world, and she knew that if Veronica even so much as glanced in the general direction of the sink, she would *know*.

That is, if she didn't know already.

With a pale finger, Anne swirled the basin, trying desperately to make the seeds sink to the bottom. Then she finally went to the door.

A deep breath, remembering that her daughter was here and that whatever happened she would have to protect her, and then Anne made her entire face go slack. She used the finger that she had swirled the water in the basin to put a few drops of the dirty liquid on her forehead. Then she pulled the door open a few inches.

A dark hazel eye stared back at her.

"Veronica?" Anne said, intentionally making her voice crack.

"Anne," the woman responded. Her lips were a tight line on her face—not a good sign. "Can I come in?"

Anne braced the door with her shoulder.

"Oh, no. I think I'm coming down with something, I—I wouldn't want you to catch it," she replied. Anne followed this up with a small cough into her curled hand.

Too far; don't be fake.

"That's alright, I'll only be a minute."

Veronica put a hand on the door and gently applied pressure to it. Anne resisted.

"No, really, Veronica. I wouldn't want you to catch this."

There was a moment of silence.

Go home, please, just go home.

But Veronica had other ideas. The woman's shoulders relaxed.

"Anne, please, I have to ask you something—you wouldn't want me to come back with Ken, would you?"

An image came to mind of the last time she had seen the man, his hairy barrel chest glistening in the hot sun, his face red with the 'shine. He had snickered at her then, and she even thought that he had thrust his britches in her direction.

She hadn't liked the way that he had looked at her, especially with Teresa at her side.

"Didn't think so," Veronica said, and this time when she pushed the door, Anne stepped out of the way.

Chapter 4

"Is Teresa napping?" Veronica asked as she took Anne's seat at the head of the table.

"Yes," Anne lied, hoping that her daughter was busy with her imaginary friends and didn't overhear them. It wouldn't go over well if she came roaring out of her room and proved Anne a liar.

If there were two things that the citizens of the swamp despised, it was liars and thieves.

And witches, of course, but everyone hated witches.

"I don't mean to be rude, but I am feeling rather ill. Is there something that I can help you with, Veronica?"

The woman pressed her lips together again and crossed her legs.

"Well," Veronica began, making a duck face. "When I have company, I usually offer something to drink. Tea, perhaps?"

"Yes, of course," Anne said quickly, turning to the stunted lantern beside the basin that contained the tomato seeds. She made her way towards it, trying not to draw Veronica's gaze.

Despite her best efforts, Anne couldn't help it and looked in anyway, hoping that the seeds were gone. It took all of her effort to suppress a sigh when she saw only a murky gray.

Better than seeds, but it was probably best if Veronica didn't see the dirty water, either.

Anne lit a match and set fire to the small tin of kerosene. It ignited immediately, and she took an involuntary step backward. After what had happened to her husband, she didn't much care for fire. Her eyes darting around the room, she found the container with less than a liter of well water left in it. She had meant to use it to soak some of Teresa's more soiled clothing—specifically the clothes that she had dirtied while Anne had been on the porch swing dreading this exact moment—but Veronica Thomas was perhaps the most influential woman in the swamp. She and her husband Ken were of good stock, their families having been in Stumphole for more years than even the town historian—a tiny fellow by the name of Randall Mason—could recount.

If the woman wanted tea, she would be served tea.

Anne swallowed hard, her mind racing as she filled the metal kettle with the last of her water. It would mean another long hike to get more, but that was okay. If she went on the hike, it would mean that Veronica didn't know that it was her who had stolen the produce.

"I only have Earl Gray," she said, her back still to Veronica. "Is that okay?"

"Well, if that's the only thing you have, I suppose that it *has* to be okay, doesn't it?"

"I'm—I'm sorry," Anne stammered. "I just don't have much anymore. After Wallace—"

"Earl Gray is fine," Veronica interrupted. "But that's not why I'm here."

Anne froze again.

"Someone was in my garden the other night, Anne. They stole my vegetables."

For the second time that day, Anne had a hard time breathing. Her mind flicked to the other night, when she had seen first the match in the window, then the light.

And then the eyes; Veronica's eyes.

Is this a trick? Did she see me, and now she's testing me?

Anne was at a loss for what to say or do.

Deny? Run? What?

Thankfully, Veronica spoke again, clearing some of the air.

"I know, I was shocked too. I thought I saw someone leaving with a bag full of vegetables, but I couldn't tell who it was. Bastard stole a lot of food."

Anne allowed herself another breath—just a small one.

"That's—"

The kettle whistled and Anne jumped.

"You okay?"

Anne took the kettle off the flame and then blew it out.

"Fine," she said. "Just a little sensitive to noise, what with this illness and all. I'm sure it's nothing, though."

Veronica grunted.

"Anyway, I was just coming by to all the houses to let people know that there is a thief out there somewhere, stealing vegetables. And you know with the abnormally hot weather, the crops haven't been growing that well this year."

Anne pictured the massive tomatoes, the dark green cucumbers, pumpkins so large that they sunk into the mud.

Well, if there was any consolation to be gleaned from this conversation, it was that Anne wasn't the only liar in the swamp.

"I know you don't have any vegetables of your own, but I thought I would come by and let you know as well. Just in case... in case someone steals your—steals your..."

Anne didn't let the silence become uncomfortable.

"Oh, I understand." Anne took out the tea and filled the mesh basket. As she poured the hot water over the leaves, she added, "Thank you for coming by, and I'm sorry about your vegetables. Hopefully, you have enough for the season."

Anne turned to the table with the steeping teapot in her hand and was taken by surprise when she saw that Veronica's dark brown eyes were staring directly at her. The woman's gaze was so powerful that she nearly stumbled.

"Oh, we'll have enough. Always do," she said. "And just in case someone comes by, tries to sell or trade you some vegetables, you'd be best served to decline and let me know right away. You understand, don't you?"

Anne nodded as she came back to the table.

"Of course."

She was about to place the teapot down when she noticed the squirt of dried tomato juice and seeds that had erupted from Teresa's mouth when she had bitten into the tomato.

Had Veronica seen that? Was this all some sort of game? Does she know it was me?

There was no way of knowing. Just in case, Anne put the teapot directly on top of the smear, covering almost all of it. A quick glance revealed that Veronica had taken no interest in the pot; instead, she was still staring at Anne.

Looking for any reason to break the uncomfortable stare, Anne swiveled on her heels, intending to retrieve two mugs from the counter. Except she spun too quickly and her knees buckled, sending her awkwardly to the floor. The rough wood scraped her right knee, and Anne bit her lip to avoid calling out.

"Oh, Anne," Veronica said, as she pulled herself to her feet. "You always were so *clumsy*."

"Yeah," Anne grumbled as she hobbled to the counter and grabbed the mugs.

Oh, Veronica, you've always been such a bitch.

Forcing a pained smile, Anne brought the two mugs over and was about to sit, when Veronica raised a hand.

"The milk?"

Again, Anne's heart sank. She hadn't had any cow's milk in weeks. She was about to say as much, bookended with apologies, when Veronica spoke again.

"I can't possibly have tea without milk. Be a dear and fetch me some."

Anne swallowed hard, her mind racing. Even though her illness had been a ruse, real sweat started to form on her forehead.

"Oh, yes," she said dryly.

Think, Anne. Think.

The last thing she wanted to do was upset Veronica Thomas. She could already imagine what the woman would say to the others, about how plain the inside of her house was, how she had embarrassed herself by falling, how she only had Earl Gray tea. Not having milk would definitely ruin Anne's chances of ever becoming part of that society again.

It hadn't always been this way, of course. Back when Wallace was still alive, the two of them would occasionally be invited to their dinner parties. Neither of them had a name, but because Wallace had been such a hard worker at the Mill, an exception was made. The parties themselves weren't to either of their tastes—a little too much gossip, a little too many noses and chins aimed skyward—but they had always had fun.

They'd had fun afterward, too, especially when Wallace traipsed around their house in one of Anne's slips, imitating the other women.

Anne shook these thoughts away and tried to focus on the task at hand.

She didn't have any cow's milk... the only milk she had was—

No, Anne. You can't serve her that. There's no way you can serve her that.

"Anne? Milk, please. I need milk. I can't possibly drink this"—she swirled the mug with a look of disgust on her face—"without milk."

Anne, her back still to Veronica, hesitated.

Veronica sighed, long and loud.

"Anne, what happened to you? Ever since Wallace passed, you have completely lost your social graces. It's no wonder the other women won't have you around for cards anymore."

Anne's demeanor suddenly changed; she went from nervous and afraid to seeing red.

How dare she? How dare she even mention Wallace?

So what if she didn't have any milk? With only one child—a girl, no less—and no husband, her options for making money were minimal bordering on nonexistent. The best she could manage was to trade the small scarecrow figures that she fashioned out of dried vines collected from the swamp. But that was a tiny market, one that was quickly nearing saturation.

It wasn't her fault that Wallace was dead. In fact, if anyone was to blame, it was Veronica's husband. Ken Thomas was the one who was supposed to be manning the fire extinguisher, instead of being passed out drunk on the job.

"Anne?"

"Yes, sorry," she muttered.

Her mind turned to the milk that she had expressed for Teresa and put away in the rare case that she eventually did get sick.

You want milk so badly? Fine, I'll give you milk.

She went back to the kitchen and opened one of the lower cabinets. It was still cool inside, which was a good sign.

Her milk was probably still good—*probably* still good.

She brought out the glass bottle. Like the air in the cabinet, it was cool to the touch. Then she turned and made her way back to the table, putting the bottle right next to the cup of tea that Veronica had filled—just her own, Anne noted.

The woman smiled a patronizing smile.

"That's a good girl. Maybe there is hope to get you back in with the other women yet."

But she was lying, Anne knew. There was no way she would ever be invited back.

The people of Stumphole hated thieves and witches. But they also hated single mothers. It didn't matter that Teresa hadn't been born out of wedlock. She had been labeled a single mother, and with this came a certain connotation, irrespective of the circumstances.

Anne watched as Veronica poured several ounces of milk into her mug of tea. The woman tilted the bottle toward Anne, but she shook her head.

"None for me, thanks."

"Suit yourself," Veronica said, and then blew on the warm liquid. Satisfied that it wouldn't burn her, she lowered her thin lips to the mug and took a sip.

"I hope it's to your taste," Anne added, no longer putting on a fake sick voice.

Veronica swallowed.

"Not bad, actually. Not bad at all... maybe there is hope for you yet, Anne LaForet."

Chapter 5

The food didn't last for nearly as long as Anne would have hoped. Part of it was that her rationing skills weren't as good as she had thought—mainly because she and Teresa had gone for so long without food—*real* food, and not just dry oats—that she was unable to contain herself.

Two and a half weeks.

After two and a half weeks, they were left with half of a cucumber that had gotten soft on one side, and, of course, their dreaded oats.

Like the produce, their emotions were equally as fleeting.

Those two and a half weeks had been some of the best that Anne could remember, rivaling even when Wallace had been alive. She had heard somewhere that distance made the heart grow fonder, but she was now realizing that hunger made *everything* fonder. But when the food was gone, Teresa went from rosy cheeks and smiling to pale and grumpy.

Anne didn't blame her.

In the end, as they went another week without any fruits or vegetables, their recent gorging only served to remind them of what they were missing. They had gone so long without before she had stolen the produce that they had become accustomed to eating the bland oats and whatever bitter berries she could scavenge.

After all, you can't miss what you can't remember, right?

Part of her wished she had never wandered out that night to the Thomases' when Teresa had been asleep. Part of her wished that she had taken more. And another part still wished she had wrangled Veronica's long, pale neck when she had had the gall to sit at her table, in her seat, and comment about her social graces.

Anne LaForet sighed and picked up the basin of water. It was dirty again, so dirty that it was nearly black. Dumping it meant that she would have to hike to get more, today, in the heat, but she had no choice. Everything she tried to wash just came out dirtier than when it went in.

"Terry, I'm just going to dump out the water, okay?"

Teresa was sitting in the middle of the floor, staring at the wall.

It pained Anne to see her this way, and even though the girl was only three, part of her knew that she was doing it on purpose.

"Why don't you play with the scarecrows?" she asked, indicating the twig figurines that were piled on the small end table in the corner of the room. Trading the figurines had become a near impossible task, and it seemed that she was making them more to pass the time than for the dwindling prospect of actually turning them over. To Anne, what had once looked like cute, natural ornaments had become a painful reminder of what they went without. To her, they looked like a pile of twisted, gnarled driftwood.

Anne was careful not to light the lantern anywhere near the stack of them; they would go up in seconds, she knew. And without their house?

A shudder racked Anne, and it was all she could do not to spill the water from the basin on the floor.

Without their house, the one that Wallace had built with his own hands, they really would have nothing.

She shook these negative thoughts from her mind.

At least we are healthy. At least we don't have the spots like the natives in the swamp.

"Terry? Did you hear me?"

The girl glanced up at her with her big blue eyes.

"Yes, Mom."

Disdain—how can a three-year-old be filled with disdain?

"Okay, sweetie. I'll be right back."

Anne pulled the door open with her foot and stepped out into the hot sun.

Unlike the Thomases', their house was at the back of their plot and not vice-versa. As Anne made her way past the porch swing and down the wooden steps, she gazed out over her muddy front lawn. Their plot was roughly twenty by thirty feet, with part of her land extending from the front to the side of the simple house. Marking the front of her property was a packed dirt road, and beyond that was the swamp. Stumphole Swamp—a murky bog that often filled the air with its foul regurgitations, its stinking feces, and was dotted by the tall indigenous trees that were lush with leaves. The swamp was the problem; despite the vegetation that was but a stone's throw from her house, nothing would grow on Anne's property.

She made her way to the corner of the house and squatted, preparing herself to turn the bucket over, emptying it, when her eye caught the simple white cross near one of the few trees by the side of her property.

Things would be different if you were still here, Wallace.

People, like the Veronica Thomases of the swamp, whispered that the reason why nothing grew on Anne's land was because she had buried her husband in the yard and that this had poisoned the soil. But the truth was, nothing had grown on the land even *before* Wallace had been buried. When her husband had first passed and she had made the difficult decision—the financially motivated decision—to bury him here rather than at the cemetery three miles down the packed dirt road, she had made this fact abundantly clear.

In fact, she remembered distinctly telling Veronica this very thing.

'Veronica, nothing ever *grew on my land. It's the swamp, it's too close, making the soil underneath too wet, turning all germinating seeds to rot.'*

Veronica just stared at her before a placating smile appeared on her thin lips.

'Yes, dear,' she had replied as if Anne were a child.

Shortly after this conversation, two days, maybe three, she had overheard Veronica telling her closest friends that it was Wallace's corpse that was poisoning the land, angered by the fact that there was now a husbandless woman and a child living on his property.

In hindsight, confronting her about these rumors probably hadn't been the best course of action. But that had been more than two years ago. Couldn't Veronica just forgive and move on?

Anne's mind turned to the riches of the Thomases' garden.

Would it kill the woman to bring a few fruits over once in a while? A cucumber? Tomato? After all, Anne couldn't work, not with having to take care of Teresa all the time. And Teresa was still a good number of years away from being able to work herself.

And with no crops...

Would it fucking kill her to bring me a goddamn eggplant?

Anne flipped the wash basin over, and mud splashed up from the ground and splattered her dress.

Great, now I'm going to have to wash this, too—wash this with clean water that I don't have.

Her anger surprised her, and she tried her best to calm her emotions by breathing in deeply and slowly, recalling what Wallace had told her once.

'The difference between us and them,' he had said, clearly indicating the rest of the citizens of Stumphole swamp, *'is that they react. Like animals, all they do is react. You, me, Terry? We are thinking people, Annie. Think, then act. Don't react.'*

Anne swallowed hard, fighting back tears.

If Wallace were here—

The sound of hooves on dirt drew her eyes up. A large gray mare trod carefully down the path that was the only physical separation between her property and the swamp.

It was the Thomases' horse, that much she knew, that much she recognized, but the carriage... that wasn't the Thomases'. She had never seen it before.

It was a wooden structure, simple by any measure, just four thin wheels supporting a wooden frame with large beige cushions, but it was *new*. And new things rarely appeared in the swamp.

I wonder—

But the horse suddenly stopped, and the door to the carriage burst open.

"Anne!" Veronica shouted as she stepped out. She had to hike up her dress—a brilliant white laced outfit, also new, it appeared—to make sure it didn't make contact with the mud.

Anne couldn't help but glance down at her own soiled dress. The grimace remained plastered on her face.

"Anne! I have the greatest news!"

Anne tried to feign a smile as she stood, but failed.

Did you come here to bring Wallace back from the dead?

Chapter 6

"Veronica? What can I do for you?"

Anne dropped the empty basin, making sure not to step in the soft mud where the dirty water had soaked in.

The woman said nothing—instead, she walked over, dress still hiked high, her steps large, her gait bouncy, joyful even.

"Veronica?"

The driver sitting at the front of the carriage stared straight ahead, both the horse and man stoic and unmoving.

What the hell is going on?

A quick dart toward the window showed that Terry was still inside, but instead of looking at the wall, she was now playing with one of the scarecrow figurines.

The sight made Anne smile.

They didn't have much, but they had each other, which had to be good for something, didn't it?

"Anne? Anne! Over here!" Mrs. Thomas waved. It was all Anne could do to avoid rolling her eyes. The woman was less than twenty paces away; announcing her presence was hardly necessary.

"Yes?"

Veronica hustled over, her face starting to redden with the effort, sweat forming on her brow. It made Anne feel good to see this woman, a woman who likely hadn't worked a day in her entire wife, put considerable effort into something, even if it was only to bound across her muddy lawn.

"Please," she huffed, grabbing Anne by the arm. "We need to go inside. I have great news."

"But the—"

Basin, she wanted to say, but Veronica's grip was strong and she yanked Anne through the thick mud.

"Don't worry about that; I have *great* news, please, you must hear it right away."

At least it's not about the stolen produce, Anne thought as she allowed herself to be pulled back into her home.

"Tea, Anne. Remember last time?"

Anne bit her tongue.

"Yes, of course. Right away." She hurried to the counter and again lit the burner. It was like *déjà vu*; their interaction was so similar to the last time Veronica had been by less than a month ago.

That came as no surprise, though; Veronica always treated her the same way. And it was all Anne could do to not lash out at her. After the stolen fruits and vegetables had been consumed, Terry wasn't the only one that had become short-tempered.

It wasn't Anne's fault; hunger had the capacity to make anyone short.

"What's the great news, Veronica?" Anne asked with her back to the woman, waiting for the last of their fresh water to boil in the kettle.

"News?" Terry repeated. Now that there was little to no chance that Veronica was here to accuse them of stealing the produce, Anne felt no need to send her to her room. It was fine to be in the kitchen playing with the wooden figurines, provided she listened to Anne's instructions: for no reason whatsoever was she to mention any of the food—the tomatoes, cucumbers, or squeaky eggplant—that they had eaten.

Veronica sighed so deeply that Anne turned, concern on her face. The woman's gaze was downcast, her head casting a shadow over the table.

Anne immediately moved toward the woman.

"Veronica? You okay? Veron—"

Veronica raised her head, the massive smile on her face giving Anne pause. A thin-lipped woman to begin with, smiling the way she was now, it looked like her lips had entirely disappeared and she was all teeth. Big, white teeth. Teeth like the horse's outside.

If it weren't for the woman's shining brown eyes, Anne would have thought the look sinister as opposed to one of complete and unadulterated joy.

"I'm pregnant," she said simply.

Anne nearly dropped the mug in her hand.

"Wh—what?" she stammered.

For all of Mrs. Thomas's makeup and hair and pomp and circumstance, Anne knew that she was well past her child-bearing years. Back around the time when Wallace died, there had been rumors going around the swamp that Ken Thomas was frustrated that Veronica was unable to bear a child. No children meant that there were fewer hands to work, be it gardening, at the Mill, or at the blacksmith's. The rule of the swamp was that the more children you had, the more prosperous you were. Having many children was not only a way to ensure financial stability, but also to continue the Thomas name. Anne herself had once begged Wallace to try for a boy, knowing the facts as she did, but Wallace had wanted to wait.

And, well, that hadn't worked out, had it?

But now Veronica... she must have been near forty, and pregnant?

"You can close your mouth, dear," Veronica said, but she was still grinning.

Anne's jaw snapped shut.

"Really?" she whispered.

"Oh, now you're just being rude. How about that tea, hmm?"

Anne glanced at the floor.

"I'm sorry," she said meekly. "Congratulations. I know that Ken wanted a child."

The response was cold and immediate.

"Who told you that?"

Anne was in the process of turning back to the kettle, which had started to whistle and whine, but the viciousness of the question caused her to freeze.

"Anne? Who told you that Ken wanted another child?"

"No one, I—I—I—it's just that Wallace wanted another child, a boy, you know, so I thought—"

"You thought? You *thought*? Do yourself a favor, Anne, and don't think. Ken is *not* Wallace. You'd do well to remember that."

Anne swallowed hard and turned back to the kettle, taking it off the heat. Some of the steam billowed up to her face, but she barely felt it.

Her face was hot already.

How dare she? Come in here, treat me like I'm a child?

Anne ground her teeth.

To come in here and tell me that Ken isn't Wallace. No shit; Wallace was ten times the man that Ken will ever be.

"Anne? The tea?"

Anne poured the near boiling water over the tea leaves and turned back to Veronica, plastering a weak smile on her face.

"Almost ready."

"Good," Veronica said, the corners of her lips turning up again. "And then you are going to tell me how you did it."

Anne put the pot on the center of the table and sat down.

"Tell you how I did what, Veronica?"

"Tell me how you did *it*."

The fake smile fell off Anne's face and she stared, stupefied.

"Oh, don't give me that look. You told me a moment ago that you knew Ken wanted another child, and—"

"No, I didn't—"

Veronica held up a hand, immediately silencing her.

"For more than ten years, we've tried. Every month it was the same, during my blood; we did the same thing over and over again. But nothing worked. I was afraid that he would—well, never mind about that. It doesn't matter now. What matters is that I came here a month ago—to your house, Anne—and that is the only thing that I did differently before I got pregnant."

Her eyes flicked to the pot of tea, while Anne just continued to stare.

What the hell does this have to do with me?

"Earl Gray, you say?"

Anne nodded slowly.

"Yes..."

"Hmm. Well, you *are* going to tell me how you did it."

An awkward silence fell over them both. Eventually, Anne broke it.

"I'm really not—"

Veronica sighed heavily.

"Look, Anne. You're going to tell me what you did, or else I'll have Ken come and give you a talking to for all the fruits and vegetables you stole from our garden."

Chapter 7

The only thing that spread faster than disease in the swamp was rumors. And Anne would've argued that the latter might actually be more dangerous.

At first, however, she couldn't believe her luck. As Veronica's belly grew, so did the baskets of fruits and vegetables that mysteriously arrived on Anne's doorstep. And this all came after Veronica forced her to tell her the truth about the tea.

At first, Anne had denied everything.

Nothing, it was just Earl Grey.

No, just water. Water and milk and tea.

The tea was from the market—traded two wooden scarecrows for it.

No, the mug was clean.

But Anne couldn't hold out forever, and eventually, the constant threats of the drunk Ken Thomas visiting, especially with Terry sitting and playing silently on the floor in plain view, broke her down. The truth about the milk came out, as embarrassing as it was. *'A coincidence,'* Anne said between apologies, but Veronica was having none of it. When the fancy women started to eyeball her, Terry, and the scarecrow figurines, all hinting in not so many words of witchcraft, Anne did the only thing she could: she latched on to the idea that her breast milk was some sort of magical elixir. And when Veronica stopped visiting and instead sent her horse with the same thin driver to drop off a basket overflowing with produce every week, who was she to complain?

And then, as predicted, especially considering the socialite that was Veronica Thomas, Anne's 'magical elixir' rumor spread. It wasn't long before Christine Porsette came by, eyes downcast, cheeks red with either wine, embarrassment, or both, mumbling something about being unable to conceive. Anne's initial reaction was to deny everything, to send the woman home. But that was before Christine produced two silver pence coins from behind her back.

What could Anne say to that?

Thinking of Terry, Anne said what came most natural. She wouldn't make any promises, but she would give Christine some of her milk, as she had Veronica. She went on to add some instructions, which were essentially a rehashing of Veronica's experience: drink the milk, go home, and then lay with her husband during her blood.

And then Christine left, gone on her merry way, her cheeks no longer red, her face no longer twisted in a frown.

Although Anne didn't hear the words from Christine's mouth, rumors, if they were to be believed, suggested that the woman was indeed pregnant.

While Christine was the second woman, Patricia was the third. And her story was much the same, only this time Anne asked for three pence, which were promptly paid. And unlike Christine, Patricia, her smile so wide that it pained Anne just to look at her, returned less than a month later with another pence.

She too, like Veronica and Christine before her, was pregnant.

Anne was skeptical — *'Thinking people,'* Wallace had said, *'me, you, and Terry are thinkers'* — but the proof was in the mud, as the saying went in Stumphole.

When Susan, Margie, and Laura all came and drank her milk, paying subsequently larger sums with each visit, and they all became pregnant in time, Anne started to believe.

She believed that perhaps there was a life for her and Terry after Wallace. After all, the money that she had made in three or four short months was more than Wallace had pulled in working two full years at the Mill.

And so Anne spent most of her days on the porch swing, listening to the rare breeze that rustled the leaves above amidst the sounds of the swamp and the creaking of the chains that held the swing to the wooden roof.

So many women visited Anne on a weekly basis that she had commissioned the local potter to come up with a ceramic device that cupped over her breast to help express the milk into containers. There were so many bottles in her cupboard that she had to label them to make sure she didn't give the very old ones to any of her more important clients.

Suffice it to say, the milk business ran well in Stumphole for a while.

The present day was cooler than most, and Anne was forced to wear her new sweater, a white wool sweater that was made specifically for her, with buttons on the chest so that the front could be pulled down to expose her breast. The air was cool, but the sun was still warm on her skin. Which was all fine for Anne, as she always felt a little warm when expressing.

As she sat on the swing with the ceramic device cupping her right nipple, she heard Terry talking to herself inside. A quick peek through the window revealed that the girl, not quite four yet, was playing with the scarecrows, talking to herself. Anne had started giving these away to each of the women she helped along with the milk, as a sort of calling card. She only had maybe a dozen left.

Terry was running out of toys to play with.

Anne couldn't help the smile that crept onto her face.

"Terry!"

Her daughter's head poked up.

"Terry, come here, would you?"

The girl scrambled to her feet and made her way to the open door, a look of concern on her face.

"What, Mom?"

The blue dress that she was wearing was crinkled at the knees.

"Terry, I told you not to kneel in that dress. If you want to kneel, put on your other pants, the ones with the holes in the knees."

The girl made a face.

"But, Mom, it's too hot in those pants."

"Don't argue with me, Terry. Besides, it's not hot out; it's actually quite cool."

Terry just stared with her big blue eyes as if to say, *Sure, Mom.*

The smile returned to Anne's face.

"Come, sit down beside me."

Terry hesitated, but an encouraging tap was all it took to change her mind. The girl hopped up onto the bench and it immediately began to sway. Anne experienced a sharp intake of breath.

"Careful! Please, Terry, you need to be more careful!" Anne steadied the half-full bottle of breast milk at her side. "We don't want to waste any!"

Terry looked frightened, and Anne immediately regretted her reaction. After all, what did it matter if one bottle spilled? She had so many tucked away in the cool cupboard.

Anne leaned over and kissed her daughter on the forehead.

"Sorry, Terry. I didn't mean to frighten you."

For a full minute, they both just sat there, listening to their thoughts or the swamp noises, or both. When Anne felt her daughter shift uncomfortably, her patience waning, she reached behind the bench and grabbed the object that she had hidden there in one hand.

"Terry, I want you to close your eyes now, okay?"

The whine was instantaneous.

"What? Why? I don't—"

"Please, Terry."

Teresa responded by squeezing her eyes so tightly that creases formed on her forehead.

Anne shook her head.

Always so dramatic, this one.

She pulled the gift from behind the bench and laid it gently on her daughter's lap.

"Now op—"

But the girl's eyes had already snapped open. And they opened... and opened... and opened. They opened until they were so wide that Anne thought that those beautiful blue orbs might just up and fall out of her head.

"Mom!" Teresa shouted, holding the doll up to eye level. "I—I—"

Anne stroked her daughter's hair as she stared at the doll that she had had made to look just like her daughter: big blue eyes, long blonde hair. Even the dress the doll wore was fashioned after the very one that Terry currently sported.

"I love it, Mom!" Terry shouted. The girl reached over to hug Anne, and for a moment she forgot all about the milk and the contraption on her breast.

Seeing the expression of sheer joy on her daughter's face reminded her that none of that really mattered.

Anne hugged her back, hard and tight for a very long time. If it had been up to her, she would have stayed in this moment forever.

Still embraced, Anne leaned in and whispered in Teresa's ear.

"I told you, Terry. I told you things would get better after the fire—after Daddy died."

The embrace lasted a little while longer, silent tears making streaks down both their red cheeks.

Yeah, the milk business was good for Terry and Anne for a while.

Things were *really* good.

But that was before the knock at the door during the storm. That was before *she* came to visit.

Part II - An Unexpected Visitor

Chapter 8

Thunder cracked through the night sky, temporarily cutting through the sound of the rain that pelted the roof like marbles in a metal basin. Terry cried out and Anne turned toward her daughter, both of whom had awoken from the sound.

"I'm scared, Mommy," the girl whispered, her eyes wide.

Anne hushed her.

"It's just a storm, Terry. It'll be okay."

She squeezed her daughter and then held her tight, feeling the doll squish uncomfortably between their bodies. Ever since she had given it to her, the two were inseparable. Anne's scarecrow stick figures were a thing of the past, it seemed. But for once, Anne didn't seem to mind.

"Try to sleep, sweetie. Try to get some sleep; we have a big day tomorrow."

Anne wasn't just saying this to calm Terry; she had cleared her schedule, planning to take Terry to the market. Normally, this wouldn't have been considered a special occasion—they often went to the market—but this time was different. This time they actually had money to buy things.

And Anne had plans to buy *plenty* of things.

Terry squirmed in her arms.

"What about the woman at the door, Mommy?"

Anne felt her heart flutter.

"What? What woman?"

And then, as if answering her question, Anne heard a light knock on the door that was barely audible above the din of the storm. For nearly a minute, Anne remained stiff, holding Terry in her arms.

It's nothing... just the rain.

But then she heard the knocking again and knew that it wasn't the storm.

There was someone at the door.

"Mommy?"

"Shh!" Anne hushed as she pulled back the sheets and rose out of bed. "Stay here. Keep quiet."

The girl nodded, squeezing the doll even tighter now that her mother's body was no longer in the way. Sleeping in the same bed had never been meant to be a permanent thing, especially now that Terry was getting taller by the day it seemed, but Anne didn't have the heart to make her sleep alone.

The nightmares that had started after Wallace's accident, while less frequent, still reared their ugly head now and again.

"That's it, hug your doll. Everything will be okay."

Anne carefully lit the lamp and then slowly made her way out of the bedroom, listening to the rain that seemed to pelt the roof with renewed vigor.

Who is knocking so late?

It couldn't have been any of her clients... after all, she *had* cleared her schedule.

A shudder suddenly coursed through her as she passed the kitchen table.

What if something went wrong? What if Christine or Laura or one of the other girls had a miscarriage?

Anne shook her head.

She tried desperately to rationalize another reason why someone would be at her door in the middle of the night—during a thunderstorm, no less—but nothing made sense.

Cautious and alert, when Anne made it to the door, instead of opening it, she put her ear to the wood and listened.

She heard nothing.

"Who is it?" she asked quietly, her attempt at sounding strong failing miserably.

"Please," a woman's voice, one that she didn't recognize, pleaded. "Please, I need your help. I came a long way to see you, Anne. A long, long way."

Anne hesitated.

She knows my name.

"What do you want?"

"Please," the woman repeated. "Please, Anne, let me in."

There was so much sadness in her voice, such unadulterated emotion, that Anne felt compelled to open the door despite her better judgment.

What she saw was nothing like what she expected.

The woman that stood in her doorway was tall and thin, with at least three inches on Anne. Her face was downcast, her blonde hair hanging in wet strings on her forehead. Unlike the other women that came to visit, however, Anne got the impression that it wasn't embarrassment that affected her posture so, but something else. Something more visceral.

Even looking down at her through strings of wet hair, Anne saw sadness and desperation clinging to her visible blue eye.

"Yes?" Anne asked tentatively. She glanced into the downpour and saw a horse and carriage pulled onto her muddy lawn. This woman was different, *much* different, than the other women that had visited her before. For one, Anne had never seen her horse or carriage before. And yet, even though there was nothing particularly ostentatious about either, there was just something about this woman that suggested a different class than even Veronica Thomas. She had an air of richness and aristocracy that seemed to flood off her like a strange aura.

The woman slowly raised her head, and Anne's breath caught in her throat. The woman's left eye was swollen shut, the surrounding skin a gruesome purple.

"Please," she said again, her good eye wet now from something other than rain. "I need your help."

Anne pulled the door wide and ushered her in, staring out into the storm for a moment before closing the door behind her.

Chapter 9

Anne offered the woman something warm and dry to wear, but she refused. The only thing she would accept was a seat at the table, despite the water that dripped from her soaked clothing and formed a small puddle on the floor beneath her.

After this short interaction, the two women sat in silence for some time. Twice, Anne had an inclination to say something, but the woman's stooped posture and downcast eyes convinced her otherwise.

Thinking people, not reacting people, Anne.

Instead, Anne observed. Her eyes flicked to the woman's wrists resting on her kitchen table. Both were adorned with jeweled bracelets, but not the tacky type that the Veronicas of the world liked to wear.

Everything about this woman screamed opulence without screaming anything at all.

Everything, except for her black eye.

The woman's back finally rose and she straightened as if she had just taken her first breath since arriving. Slowly, methodically, she reached into her pocket and pulled out one of Anne's wooden scarecrow figurines. She placed it standing up on the table in front of her.

Where the—?

"News travels fast and far, Anne LaForet. I heard about you all the way from Charleston."

Charleston.

Anne's heart skipped a beat. Everyone in the swamp had heard of Charleston, but to her knowledge, Anne didn't know anyone who had ever met someone from there, let alone have them sit at their kitchen table, soaked or not.

"Who is your husband?" Anne nearly whispered. She swallowed hard, trying not to let her excitement show on her face.

The woman leveled her crisp blue eye at her.

"Benjamin Heath," she said simply.

Anne did her best not to gawk.

Not only was this woman from Charleston, which housed one of the largest plantations in the entire Southeast, but she was the wife of one of the plantation's co-owners.

Anne was flabbergasted and at a loss for words. Thankfully, the woman continued speaking—Anne doubted that she would have been able to say a word even if pressed to do so.

"My name is Jane Heath," she said. "And I'm desperate. My husband and I have tried everything, but I can't get pregnant. I'm afraid—I'm afraid—"

Her voice hitched and her hand reflexively went to her bruised eye. Anne remembered the way that Ken Thomas used to holler at her, and how Veronica's dress occasionally rode up, revealing dark bruises on her arms and legs.

Yeah, Anne knew just how desperate women like Jane Heath could be.

"Please, can you help me?"

The bluntness of the question took Anne by surprise, and she took a moment to collect herself. Unlike the women from the swamp that she had helped conceive, Jane Heath represented a unique opportunity for her. Anne licked her lips, knowing that she could extract immeasurable wealth from Jane, wealth of the like that would make Veronica Thomas's stupid white dress look like it was crafted from shed snakeskin.

But Jane Heath could offer more than money.

Much, much more.

Wallace's words echoed in her head.

Me, you, Terry, we're thinking people.

Jane Heath represented more than money to Anne and Teresa; she represented a way for her to get out of the swamp, away from the Veronicas and Christines and their petty rumors and judgment.

Jane offered something that money simply couldn't buy, that even Wallace couldn't provide when he was still alive.

Jane offered *prestige*, a name.

Anne's mind was already whirring, imagining extravagant parties, Terry playing with girls her own age, tiaras and castles... a child's fairytale fantasy.

Her fantasy.

"Yes," Anne said quietly, making the difficult decision not to ask for payment of any kind. "Yes, of course, I can help."

This time, Anne couldn't help but smile.

Chapter 10

Anne LaForet awoke the day after Jane Heath's visit with a massive smile plastered on her face. She had been so excited about the possibility of leaving the swamp that sleep had been spastic, interrupted. But, surprisingly, she didn't feel tired; instead, she felt *invigorated*.

Her conversation with Jane had gone exceedingly well. The woman had drunk a full cup of tea with three ounces of her breast milk without hesitation. Desperation drove deep in this woman, and she didn't so much blink an eye at the idea of drinking the milk. Then, after an awkward embrace, she had upped and left.

Although Anne had asked for no compensation from Jane, there was an unspoken promise in the woman's good eye.

She would return, and when she did, Jane would announce her pregnancy with more than just words.

Anne just knew she would.

"Why you smiling, Mama?" Terry asked.

Anne turned to her daughter as the girl rubbed sleep from her eyes.

"I'm just happy, is all."

I'm finally happy.

It had taken a long time to get over Wallace's death, but with things looking up the way they were, Anne felt confident that she was finally free of the grief.

She still missed him, and always would, but she had to move on—and now was the time.

"I'm just happy."

Terry smiled, lifting the doll up for both of them to see.

"Mother is happy too," she said, her voice full of sleep.

Anne's brow furrowed.

"Mother?"

"Uh-huh. I'm going to call her Mother."

"The doll?"

Terry flipped onto her back and held the doll over her head by the down-filled arms.

"Yeah. Mother."

Anne shook her head, trying not to let Terry's strange name for the doll bother her. Not today; she was too happy for something like this to bother her today. Anne pulled herself out of bed, glancing quickly out the window as she did.

The rain had stopped sometime during the night and the sun was just starting to rise. Her eyes drifted across the wet grass covered in tiny spheres of rain creating prisms of light before evaporating in the morning heat. Eventually, her gaze fell on the worn white cross at the corner of her plot.

A single tear fell down her cheek, but it wasn't brought on by sadness.

We are going to be just fine, Wally. Everything is going to be just fine.

"Mom, you okay?"

Anne leaned over and tousled the girl's long blonde hair.

"Better than fine, sweetie. I'm great. Now get up and get dressed. We're going to the market, remember?"

Terry's face went flat.

"Who visited last night?" she asked.

Anne stared at her daughter's big blue eyes for a moment.

"No one," she replied after a moment's hesitation. "No one important. Now get up—we are going to get some meat today."

Terry sat bolt upright.

"*Meat?*"

Anne chuckled.

"Yep. Meat. Now get dressed, you rascal."

The Stumphole market wasn't much of a market, not really. Located in a clearing near the center of the swamp, it consisted of maybe a dozen wooden booths set up by several of the townsfolk. They weren't traditional vendors, but people of the swamp with items that they wanted to trade or sell.

The Thomases had a booth filled with produce, while Christine Porsette and her husband had one flush with grains and oats. Others still had booths with household items like bedding or candles, lanterns and fuel.

But today, as Anne made her way through the market with the smile from this morning still on her face and Terry's hand cupped in her own, she had no interest in these booths.

Today she only had eyes for one booth, the last booth, the one manned by the ever curmudgeonly Samuel Kitniss.

The meat man.

Rarely did she ever make it all the way to his booth before turning back, not wanting to deal with his scornful leer or the temptation, knowing that there was no way she could afford any of the rations of bacon or the sides of beef.

But today was different.

"Come on, Terry," she said, tugging her daughter along. "Let's go straight to the meat!"

Terry smiled and turned to her doll that was clutched in her other hand. The doll's large blue eyes rolled in her head as she shook her gently.

"You hear that, Mother? We are going to have meat!"

Anne chuckled.

They passed the Thomases' booth first, and she was surprised that Veronica was manning it instead of her husband.

"Anne!" she hollered, waving a hand. As she stood, Anne noticed that she was wearing one of her tighter dresses, a bright blue number, that accentuated her growing belly. "Interested in any produce, today?"

Anne shook her head.

"No thanks, Veronica," she replied. Anne wasn't interested in vegetables, and besides, she still hadn't finished the basket that had been mysteriously delivered last week.

Veronica had never admitted that she was the one dropping it off, but Anne knew it was her nonetheless.

Christine Porsette waved as she passed, and Anne waved back. Terry made Mother wave as well. Anne wasn't interested in interacting with any of the other booths, so she fell into the center of the worn path, filing in behind the twenty or so other patrons that perused the market this day. To her surprise, she wasn't greeted with the usual scorn; instead, people seemed to be smiling at her and little Terry. In fact, Georgia Perkins, a large, doughy woman who was always covered in flour, actually stopped to pat Teresa on the head and say hello.

Wallace, things are definitely looking up, and as you look down, I hope you are proud.

They were nearly at Mr. Kitness's meat stall when someone grabbed Anne by the arm and squeezed tightly.

"Ow!" Anne cried out, turning to see who had accosted her. She recoiled.

The woman was short, her back so crooked that she was nearly horizontal to the ground. A quick glance at the woman's hand revealed that it was a gnarled, leathery thing, the finger joints swollen and bulbous.

"Let go," she said, her voice still laced with pain.

The woman looked up. Her face was not all that indistinguishable from her hands; old, worn, and weathered. But it was her eyes that were the most off-putting. They were a dark black, the pupils unrecognizable from the irises. She reeked of rotting vegetation, which was probably—*hopefully*—emanating from the soiled rags that hung from her wire frame body.

She didn't let go. Instead, she smiled, revealing a mouth devoid of any teeth.

"Take your money and leave this place," she hissed, her voice like rustling leaves. "Take your money and flee the swamp. These people—"

Anne tried to wrench her arm away from the horrible woman that she had never seen before, but her grip held fast.

"—the people of the swamp never forget."

They were lost in the center of the throng of marketgoers now, but as Anne glanced around, she realized that no one was looking at the strange woman. Terry didn't even seem to notice her, content with muttering gibberish to her doll.

"Let go," Anne repeated, her eyes wide.

"It's not just Wallace that is buried in the swamp, Anne. There are more bodies there, and there is something evil beneath... that's why you have never been able to grow anything."

Anne looked around desperately, searching for someone to save her. She pulled again, and the woman finally let go of her arm.

"Mommy? You okay?"

Anne turned to Terry and put on a fake smile.

"Fine, just—"

She turned back to the woman, but she was gone.

"What?"

Anne looked around, trying to find her crooked outline amidst the others. She was nowhere to be found. The only evidence that she hadn't made her up was her sore arm and the lingering smell.

What the hell was that?

"Mommy?"

Anne pulled Terry quickly to the final stall.

"Nothing, Terry. I'm fine."

Mr. Kitness greeted her with his predictable frown.

"Yes?" he asked, his voice deadpan.

Anne cleared her throat, trying to put the image of the woman's crooked nose and black eyes out of her mind.

"A ration of bacon," she said quietly.

"What?"

"Bacon," she repeated. All of a sudden, the idea of meat felt less than appealing to her. It felt grotesque.

"You have money?" the man asked, eyeing her suspiciously.

Anne took a single pence out of her pocket and laid it on the wooden counter.

Mr. Kitness nodded and snatched the money before reaching beneath the stand, pulling out a thick wad of brown paper. Anne didn't even bother looking inside. She grabbed the parchment and turned to Terry.

"Let's go," she said, the smile gone from her face.

Anne refused to let the strange encounter in the swamp get to her. Not now, not when things were going so well.

It's not just Wallace buried in the swamp...

What did she know? She was a demented old lady, probably a relative of one of the women rumored to live deep within the swamp, the ones with the scabies. Or maybe *she* had scabies, for all Anne knew.

Regardless, the crooked woman knew nothing about Anne. Nothing.

Still...

Anne didn't stop at canceling her schedule for the day—she canceled it for the rest of the month, electing instead to spend time with her daughter. Before the accidental encounter with Veronica, she had spent very little time with Terry—really *with* her. Instead, she used to spend nearly all of her time worrying about how they would eat that day. And the next. But now she not only had enough produce to last for weeks, but enough money to probably buy food for the rest of the year should the gifts dry up.

How much difference a single visit could make in their lives. Anne was hoping that the other visit would bring with it even more riches.

Nearly a month to the day exactly, there was another knock at the door late in the evening. A quick peek out the window revealed a horse and carriage; plain, but clearly not from the swamp.

It was Jane, she knew, which was why her smile was big and broad when she pulled the door open. Upon seeing the woman, however, any expression of glee fell off her face.

"My God, are you okay?" she asked in a whisper.

Jane's head was bowed, her blonde hair covering her face. And yet despite the woman's obvious efforts to conceal her face, Anne couldn't help but notice the purple welts that peeked through.

"No," Jane said hoarsely.

Anne whipped her head around to look at Terry, who was sitting on the wool rug, playing with Mother.

"Terry, can you go play in your room, please?"

The girl looked up at her, concern on her face.

"Why?"

"Terry, please, just do it."

The girl opened her mouth as if to say something else, but seeing the look on Anne's face, she quickly hopped to her feet and made her way to her room.

"And close the door, please."

Terry obliged.

Only then did Anne turn back to Jane.

"Come in," she said, stepping out of the woman's way. "Please, come in."

Chapter 11

"It doesn't always happen right away," Anne said. She tried to keep the uncertainty from her voice, but doubted she did a good job of it. The truth was, she really had no idea how any of this worked. After all, she was just a simple girl from the swamp without a name.

As she sat across from the woman nursing the tea in front of her, she realized that she had grossly underestimated the extent of Jane's bruises when she had first arrived.

Her right eye, the one that had been bruised when she had visited a month ago, had turned a sour yellow, but now the other eye was bruised nearly as badly. And there was a cut on her lip, a deep cut. When Jane spoke, she did so with a slight lisp, which Anne figured was either to cover up the fact that one of the front teeth in her lower jaw was missing or that it was caused by the missing tooth itself.

"How many times will it take?" Jane asked meekly.

Anne thought about it for a moment. With all the other girls—nine, she counted—drinking the tea had been a one-shot success. It hadn't occurred to her that it might take more than one attempt. Rather than answer with an ambiguous response, she changed the subject.

"Are you sure you aren't pregnant?"

Jane nodded.

"Got my blood yesterday."

Anne chewed her lip, trying to decide how to proceed. Jane saved her the trouble by standing and hiking up her dress. At first, Anne looked away, thinking that the woman was going to prove to her that she was in fact bleeding, but when Jane spoke next, Anne quickly looked back.

"And when Benjamin found out, he did this."

Anne cringed.

There was a red welt that ran all the way across her stomach. The wound—from a horse whip, maybe?—became progressively deeper as it went from left to right across her pale belly, and the last three inches on the right side were still bleeding.

"Jesus," Anne whispered as she started to stand. "Let me get you something to clean that up."

Jane stayed her by raising a hand.

"No, please, sit. It's not that bad."

Anne obliged.

"Tell me how many times it will take."

"I—I—I am not sure," Anne stammered. "Three, maybe?"

Jane took a large gulp of the tea that Anne had mixed with four ounces of breast milk.

"Three," Jane repeated, more to herself than to Anne.

"Maybe two. This could be the time."

Jane swallowed another gulp, her lips turning down at the ends.

"He—he is having sex with other women," she admitted quietly. "I know he is. He says he isn't, but I smell their perfume on him. I can literally taste them when he kisses me."

Jane made a disgusted face and Anne cringed involuntarily. She felt bad for this woman then, bad that she had only pictured her as a means to her own end. But then she thought of Terry and how they had eaten oats and only oats for so long that she couldn't even look at them now without gagging.

There was no way that she would ever go back to that.

And then there was the woman at the market, the old crone that had insisted that she take Terry and leave.

Anne shuddered and tried to stay focused.

"He's getting more and more angry—and more violent. He can't even look at me without cursing. I'm afraid... I'm afraid that..."

She let her words trail off, and it was just as well. Anne knew where this line of dialogue was headed, and it would do neither of them any good to say the words out loud.

"Drink your tea, Jane. Drink your tea, and I'm sure that this time everything will be okay. That this time you will get pregnant."

Chapter 12

Anne was made a liar.

A month to the day, she heard that same quiet knock at her door. But this time when she spotted the horse outside, the shadow of a driver, slumped ever so slightly, her spirits didn't lift.

Instead, her heart sank.

"Terry, go to your room."

They were in the middle of dinner, stewed tomatoes and potatoes with celery, and the girl was still chewing.

"Can't I finish, Mom?" she asked with a mouthful of food.

Anne shook her head.

"No. Go to your room now," she said more forcefully than she had intended. The girl swallowed, grabbed her doll from the table, and quickly went to her room.

With a deep breath, Anne made her way to the door and pulled it open.

Jane's arm was broken. Anne could tell by the way the woman was holding it close to her body, bent, pressed protectively to her chest.

Her broken nose was more obvious: both eyes were black, but unlike her previous black eyes, the discoloring spread from the cut on the bridge of her nose and concentrated beneath her eyes. The nose itself, previously Parisian and true, had a slight depression in the area of the cut, and continued a little to the left.

For some reason, the bent nose reminded her of the strange woman from the market, and Anne felt an icy chill travel up and down her spine.

Wallace isn't the only one buried here—you should leave.

"Can I—?" Jane broke into a phlegmy cough. The motion caused her broken arm to bounce, and she cried out in agony.

It pained Anne just to look at her.

"Come in, come in," she whispered.

There was no small talk or idle chitchat this time; there was nothing that needed saying. Jane's eyes did enough talking.

She was frightened for her life.

Why isn't it working? Why isn't she getting pregnant? What the hell is going on?

"This is the third month," Jane said at last, her words coming out with too much air. The woman didn't even bother to disguise the fact that the incisors on her lower jaw were gone. All told, Jane Heath was a shadow of the woman that had first arrived, even with her eye swollen shut at the time. Three months ago, she had exuded an aura of prestige, of wealth, but now the only thing coming off Jane was the reek of fear and pain.

Anne swallowed hard.

"I know."

She offered the woman more tea, but Jane refused.

"You have to drink," Anne said. "You have to drink the tea."

Jane shook her head.

"No, no more tea."

Anne hesitated, confused by the woman's words.

Was she giving up? Was that it? What would Benjamin do to her? *And if she has given up, what is she doing here?*

This last thought came with an overwhelming sense of fear. If Benjamin had inflicted such pain on his own wife, what might he do if he found her here, with Anne? What might he do to Terry?

No, she can't give up. It'll take just one more time, that's it. One. More. Time.

Thoughts of Veronica Thomas drifted into her mind. The frightful experience with the old crone had kept her away from the market for nearly a week, but the bacon had been so good, so ridiculously delicious, that no feeling of unease was capable of keeping her away. And when she had gone back to the market, she'd seen Veronica. The woman had given birth to a beautiful blonde girl—Harmony—and the entire Thomas clan had been at their booth. Even Ken Thomas, who had been *actually* smiling, had seemed elated. They'd appeared so happy that it warmed Anne's heart; after all, her milk had done this.

She had done this.

But it hadn't always been that way for the Thomases. There had been a time that Veronica had been scared like Jane. In the swamp, having children meant everything.

And evidently the same was true for Jane... or at least for her husband.

Anne waited for her next instruction, but Jane seemed content with staring at the table before her. It was as if she were analyzing every nook, every crevice, for some unseen treasure—or a way to escape, to burrow deep inside one of those infinitesimal separations of wood grain and hide.

Anne knew this, because after Wallace had died, she had felt much the same way. But she had had Terry to pull her out of her funk, a luxury that Jane didn't have.

At least not yet.

Slowly, Jane raised her eyes.

"No, no tea," she repeated. "Just the milk."

Anne nodded, pleased that Jane hadn't given up after all. She quickly went to the cupboard and retrieved a four-ounce bottle of milk. She placed it on the table before Jane, but the woman with the bruised and battered face didn't immediately grab it and drink it down as Anne expected, as she had done with the tea on her previous visits. Instead, she stared at it much like she had stared at the tabletop.

"Jane? You okay?"

Jane looked up at her and again shook her head.

"No, not the bottle, either."

Anne tried not to let exasperation leak into her voice.

"What, then?"

"From the source, Anne. I want milk from the source."

Anne's brow furrowed in confusion.

The source?

Then she followed the woman's gaze down to her own chest. Realization fell over Anne.

"Uhhh," she hesitated.

She wants to suckle from my breast like a babe?

As if reading her thoughts, Jane nodded.

"Please, if I don't get pregnant this time, Benjamin is going to kill me."

It was going on two months now that Anne had refused to see any other desperate women, and she was slowly starting to regret her decision to turn them away. Not only did this impact her income, but she had detected a change in the overall feeling she was getting from others in the swamp. And Veronica parading little Harmony Thomas around wasn't helping. All eyes seemed to be on Anne when she walked through the market, but unlike before any of this had happened, they weren't staring at her with gazes full of pity or scorn. Now, they seemed filled with jealousy and... something else. Distrust, maybe? Or suspicion.

In the swamp, suspicion was bad. Very bad.

Women weren't happy that Anne had given Christine and Veronica and the other seven women the gift of a child while they were left without. Once, when she and Terry had returned from the market, there had been one of her scarecrow figurines on the porch swing, one that hadn't been there when they had left.

And it had been missing its head.

Anne swallowed hard and looked down at her blouse.

What harm could it do?

Her fingers, trembling ever so slightly, moved to the buttons and she cast a quick glance over her shoulder to see if Terry's door was still closed.

It was.

As she fumbled with the buttons, Anne felt herself nodding.

This is the time—the last time.

Chapter 13

This time the knock at the door wasn't a meek pattering.

This time it was like a massive fist hammering against the wood.

Anne jumped.

"Terry, go to—"

But she didn't even get the words out before the door was thrown wide. Terry screamed, and Anne protectively moved in front of her daughter.

As before, Jane's hair hung in front of her face, and the bruises that marked her features peeked through. Her arm, however, had either healed or she was so enraged that she didn't notice the pain. A horsewhip was clutched so tightly in her hand that her knuckles were alabaster white.

"Anne," Jane said, her eyes blazing into her. "You promised; three months at most."

She took an aggressive step forward, and Anne responded by backing up a pace. Her heel brushed against Terry's shin, who was now cowering behind her, and Anne nearly fell. She caught herself by reaching back and grabbing Terry's arm.

The girl dropped her doll.

"Hurry," Anne shouted over her shoulder. "Go to your room, close the door, and get under the bed."

Terry ran.

"You promised me," Jane hissed. She was missing more teeth now, rendering her mouth a gaping hole and her words wet and slurred. "You promised me I would have a child."

Jane took another step forward, bringing the whip in front of her at the same time.

"I didn't—" Anne began, but the whip shot out with amazing speed, sending an audible crack into the air. The tip snapped against Anne's bare forearm, immediately causing a hot red welt to rise. Anne screamed and grabbed her arm.

"Three months I have come to this shithole swamp, drinking your—"

Jane cracked the whip again, this time snapping it within inches of Anne's face. Anne, still clutching her burning arm, stumbled backward and tripped over her own feet. She fell to the floor, a gasp escaping her tight lips.

"—foul milk. But nothing... I sneak away from Benjamin every month, each time wondering if this is the month that I return only to be greeted by a shotgun."

"Please," Anne begged, tears streaming down her face. She was in agony, her arm burning, her ass throbbing from where it had struck the hardwood floor. "I didn't promise anything."

Jane took several steps forward until she was hovering directly over Anne's fallen body.

"Yes you did, you fucking slut," Jane raised the whip above her head, but hesitated before raining it down on her. "You fucking promised."

Anne heard the crack of the whip, but it moved so quickly that she didn't see it.

But she felt it. A searing pain erupted on her cheek, which was immediately followed by a spurt of blood that sprayed from her flayed face. The combination of the force of the blow and an instinctual reaction to nearly losing her eye sent Anne sprawling flat against the floor.

She didn't so much cry out as release a long, drawn-out whine.

The pain was like nothing she had ever felt before. Spit and blood dripped from her face onto the floor, but Anne did nothing to stem the flow. Instead, she shut her eyes, listening to her own breathing and Jane's huffing from cracking the whip with such ferocity. Eyes still closed, Anne screamed as loud and as long as she could. Then she sucked in another breath.

"I didn't promise anything!" she yelled hoarsely. "I didn't fucking promise anything!"

She opened her eyes and stared at the floor, which was so close that she couldn't focus. Another sound made her wince, but when it wasn't accompanied by searing pain, Anne realized that it wasn't the whip.

It was a door.

No!

Anne flipped onto her back and leveled her eyes at the room that she and her daughter shared. Terry's round face, her blue eyes wet with tears, looked at her from between the two-inch-wide opening.

"Ter—" she started, but blood filled her mouth and she had to spit before continuing. "Terry, close the door! *No matter what, don't come out of your room!*"

The girl hesitated, which was just enough time for Jane to notice her.

"You have a daughter? What gives you the *right* to have a daughter? A piece of trash like you, from the *swamp*, of all places, while I, Jane Heath, can't have one? Huh? What gives you the *right*?"

Terry slammed the door closed.

"Please," Anne stammered.

"Please what? I should *take* your daughter—I deserve a child more than you."

"No!"

Jane snapped the whip again, and this time it shredded not only Anne's cotton nightgown, but the skin on her back as well. Anne's spine inverted from the shock, and her mouth opened wide in a croak.

The pain was so intense that she thought she might pass out.

"Roll over," she heard someone hiss; someone far, far away. "Roll over or I'll whip you again."

Anne, eyes turned backward in their sockets, managed to somehow flip onto her back. Only her shoulder blades and tailbone made contact with the wood floor; the simple thought of placing an inch of her flayed skin against the wood was enough to bring on a fresh bout of nausea.

Jane was suddenly on top of her, yanking her nightie down, tearing the expensive fabric like toilet paper. Anne's pale breasts spilled out from the enlarged neck hole.

She closed her eyes again, this time allowing the darkness to close in on her, and as she did, Anne heard a distinctive sound.

A *suckling* noise.

And then she passed out.

Chapter 14

The ground was wet and soft, coating Benjamin Heath up to the elbows in mud. When he had taken a horse and followed his wife earlier that day, he had envisioned this going a little differently. He definitely hadn't thought that he would be half buried in mud with Jessie Radcliffe lying beside him, grumbling about how badly the swamp reeked. If Jane was having an affair, as he suspected she was, he half wanted it to be with one of the assholes in Charleston, one of the men that paraded around town like some sort of human peacock draped in silk and adorned with gems and jewels. It would be much more enjoyable inflicting pain on someone like that. But here? In the swamp? Shit, he expected that these inbred fuckers lived on pain.

"Shut up," Benjamin mumbled. "There's something happening... I can see... I can—"

The truth was, he couldn't see much. He caught a glimpse of the top of his wife's head, and that of another, dark-haired woman. The second woman had turned briefly to the window at one point, and for a second he thought that she had spotted him. When she turned her back to him a moment later, Benjamin realized that she hadn't.

But that face... it wasn't one he recognized.

What the hell is Jane doing here? And who the fuck is that?

"What's she doin'?" Jessie asked.

"I said, *shut up*," Benjamin hissed. Jessie might have been his best friend, his closest confidant, and his loyal accomplice, but the man's constant chatter was infuriating.

This was the third time that Benjamin had spotted his bitch wife leaving in the afternoon when she thought that he was having his afternoon nap.

He wasn't napping, of course. The mid-afternoon nap was just a ruse to give Jessie the opportunity to sneak the girls in through the back. Unlike that bitch Jane, he could do whatever he wanted to these girls and they never complained, never smart-mouthed him or stepped out of line. Sure, Jessie paid them off, but what did that matter? He never saw any money changing hands.

Benjamin nearly chuckled at the thought of how much money Jessie probably had to pay for the last one.

The image of their young bodies, their wet tongues making tracks all over his body as he lay splayed, blindfolded, his arms tied to the bedposts, made the front of his trousers suddenly feel a little too tight.

If Jane wouldn't give him a baby, wouldn't give him a chance for the honored and revered and feared Heath name to live on, well then, he would plant one in one of these nubile beauties.

Or *they* would die trying.

Two months ago during one of his "naps," he had overheard the sound of horse hoofs on the cobble walk out front of his palatial estate. Nobody left in the afternoon, not without his permission, and *especially* not with one of his horses. His initial demands to be untied had gone unheeded, probably because the girls had assumed it was all part of the game. A strong bite to one of the girls' inner thighs, a bite so strong that it had left him with a mouthful of smooth skin and sinew, had let them know that he was serious.

Benjamin had made it to the window just in time to see the carriage pulling onto the road. When it hadn't returned until late that night, and he couldn't find Jane anywhere in the estate, he'd known what was up. The bitch was cheating on him—that was the only thing that made sense.

That night, he had beaten his wife harder than usual, before planting his seed inside her over and over again. Yet he'd never asked her where she had gone; he knew better. If he asked outright, even if he asked with his fists and feet, she would clam up and never tell him.

Fucking stubborn bitch.

If anything, he preferred it this way. If he caught her in the act with another man, then he would be justified in killing them both—in giving them both what they deserved.

"Can't see shit," Benjamin mumbled. He pulled himself out of the mud to get a better look, which also served to alleviate the uncomfortable feeling in his balls from lying on his erection. "Stay here, Jessie."

Jessie hesitated in the prone position, his hands buried in the mud as he stopped mid-pushup. The man was tall and lanky with a narrow face to match and shaggy brown hair that covered his forehead. He looked like some sort of oversized swamp bug emerging from the mud. The man's thin lips opened, but Benjamin pre-emptively stopped him before he spoke.

"Shut the fuck up, Jessie."

The man's mouth snapped shut. Friend or not, he knew better than to test Benjamin's wrath. Nobody from Charleston was stupid enough to contradict Benjamin Heath.

On his haunches now, Benjamin ambled closer to the window. From his new vantage point, he could make out more of his wife's outline, but her back was to him. Peering through her arms and legs, he thought he saw the other woman lying on the floor in front of her.

What the fuck is going on?

Of all the scenarios that had run through Benjamin's head as he'd watched the carriage make its way out the gate, Jane visiting a *woman*, of all people, had not been one of them.

What is she doing?

He moved a little bit closer, and then his breath caught in his throat.

Jane jumped on top of the woman, tearing at her blouse, revealing large, soft breasts with dark nipples.

As he watched, Benjamin's expression went from shock to confusion.

But then the corners of his lips turned up.

Oh, this is good. This is *real good.*

PART III - Spilled Milk

Chapter 15

The people of the swamp never forget, the old crone's voice echoed in Anne's head.

Her eyes snapped open, and she immediately wondered how long she had been out.

It could have been minutes, but it could have also been hours. There was no way to know.

Her back hurt, her face hurt, her arm hurt, and her breasts hurt. She tried to lift her face off the floor, but it didn't budge. Fear coursed through her, as she thought that perhaps Jane was still here, that her palm was pushing her face against the floor.

But when she tried to raise her head again, her heart rate slowed. Jane wasn't holding her head to the floor; instead, her blood had started to congeal and it was causing her face to stick to the wood.

With one hard yank, the skin on her cheek stretched but eventually broke free, ungluing itself from the floor.

She was crying, she realized then, but it wasn't from the pain—or, at least, it wasn't *all* from the pain. Jane had gone from a potential friend, someone who could not only provide her with the means for her and Terry to leave to the swamp, to start a new life, but also offer prestige, to someone that wanted to kill her.

Kill.

Barely holding back a grunt of pain, she managed to force herself into a sitting position. Her eyes were wide, frantic, fearing that at any moment Jane would reveal herself and finish the job. After another uneventful minute, she realized that that wasn't going to happen.

The door had been left wide open, and Anne could see all the way to the packed dirt road.

Jane and the horse and carriage had fled. And along with them any prospect of Anne and Teresa ever leaving the swamp.

Only now did she dare inspect the damage that the crazed, desperate woman had inflicted on her.

Her probing fingers revealed a deep gash that ran from just in front of her ear to the corner of her lip. The skin separated when she ran her fingers over it, sending a shudder up and down her spine. Blood still wept from the wound, and she knew that it was in her best interest to stem the bleeding and try to force the two sides together, otherwise it would scar. But she was only kidding herself. She had fixed up enough cuts on Wallace's hands when he worked at the Mill to know that a cut this deep was going to scar no matter what she did about it.

She turned her attention to her breasts next, wincing when she saw how red and sore her nipples were. She had passed out just as Jane had started suckling from them, but she knew that the woman had pulled on them hard—so hard that she felt as if she had been punched in the chest.

And maybe she had.

Anne closed her eyes and continued to weep, her thoughts turning to the day when she had hidden behind the Thomases' house, building up the courage to steal some produce for her and Terry to eat—to survive. And then she was in her kitchen, angrily pouring breast milk in Veronica's tea. Her next thought was of the first time that Jane had shown up to her door, her eye swollen, her posture stooped.

What happened? How did it come to this?

The sound of creaking wood drew Anne out of her own head. At first, she thought that it was Terry coming out of her room again, and she whipped around, instructions to keep the door closed, to hide under her bed, on the tip of her tongue.

But the bedroom door was still closed.

As her head swiveled around slowly, her heart kicked into high gear.

At some point during her struggle with Jane, the lamp closest to the door had gone out, leaving only the one at the far end of the room behind her to illuminate the interior of her small house. And with the figure in the doorway blocking any moonlight from entering, she could only make out their outline.

"No," Anne said, her vision still blurry from the tears that continued to fall. "I didn't promise anything. I—"

But a laugh cut her off.

It wasn't Jane—it was a man's laugh, low and gruff.

And *mean*.

"Please," Anne begged.

Was it Ken Thomas? Had Veronica heard the commotion and sent him over to check on her?

"Help me."

The man laughed again.

And then he spoke, and Anne knew instantly that it wasn't Ken Thomas. Even though she had never heard his voice before, she was fairly confident she knew who it was.

And this realization made her blood turn to ice in her veins.

"I knew that *bitch* Jane was cheating on me. But with a woman?" Anne couldn't tell if it was incredulity or sarcasm that crept into his voice. "A woman from the swamp? A fucking *commoner?*"

He took a large step into the room, and then another. He had a huge gait, traversing all the way to the kitchen in just two strides.

"Please," Anne begged. "I didn't promise anything. I'm sorry, I didn't—we didn't—"

Benjamin Heath took another step forward, finally moving into the dim glow from the lantern.

For the second time in only a minute, Anne felt unable to breathe.

Benjamin Heath was tall and thin and *nude*. The man's cock that hung between his legs was partially erect, and it swayed from side to side with every step. But despite this horrific sight, it was his hands that had the most profound effect on Anne. They were balled into knobby fists, the multitude of scars on his knuckles oddly clear in the poor lighting.

Anne pictured Jane's wounds, the broken nose, the black eyes, and she knew that unlike Wallace's, Benjamin's scars weren't from any mill—they were from his wife's face. And if he had done that to his own wife, there was no telling what he would do to her—in his words, *a commoner from the swamp*.

Sensing danger, Anne's reactive biological instincts took over, but it wasn't in her to fight or flee. Anne's programming was to freeze. It was as if she had been suddenly transported out of her body and was now hovering overhead as Benjamin finally strode over to her. One of his large hands extended with amazing speed, his open palm slapping her bloody cheek, reigniting the pain. Anne's head flew backward and the base of her skull smacked against the hard floor.

"Fucking peasant blood," Benjamin muttered, wiping his hand on his thigh, leaving a red smear behind. "So Jane likes these breasts, doesn't she? Well, let's see what I can do about that."

The man lowered himself on top of her, and she felt his now rock-hard penis graze against the inside of her leg. He yanked her dress with such force that it tore away completely, leaving her naked and shivering on the floor. Then Benjamin lowered his head and she felt warmth and wetness on her breast again. Only this time, unlike Jane, it was gentle, his tongue lightly flicking her raw nipple.

And then his teeth clamped down and he pulled.

Anne screamed, and he entered her with a grunt.

When it all ended, Benjamin let out a final, prolonged groan and then slid out of her. Sweat dripped profusely from his face and landed on her like rain.

Anne's eyes were open, or at least she thought they were. She couldn't be sure, given that she was unable to focus on anything, could only make out amorphous shapes.

"'Atta girl," Benjamin said breathlessly. "Now I can see why Jane keeps coming back to you."

He chuckled and pulled himself to his feet, leaving Anne lying on her back. As he moved toward the door, Anne allowed herself the hope that this nightmare was finally over.

Please be done, she thought as her body curled into a ball, her thumb making its way to her mouth.

Benjamin continued to chuckle.

"Ah, like a babe. The babe that Jane can never give me."

Somewhere in her subconscious, Anne realized that he continued to make his way to the open door.

It is over.

But when the man spoke again, she knew that she was mistaken.

"Jessie, get your skinny ass out of the mud and come over here. It's your turn."

Anne cringed, but lacked the faculties to do anything else.

Passing in and out of consciousness, she barely acknowledged that someone else, someone even taller and thinner than Benjamin Heath, was on top of her.

It lasted only minutes, and then that too was over.

Anne couldn't even manage to pull herself into the fetal position anymore. Her body was racked with pain, from her face to her breasts to between her legs.

"What do we do now?" she heard a voice say. It was indistinct, coming from nowhere and everywhere at the same time.

She heard the sound of a match igniting, then caught a flash of light behind her closed lids.

Anne opened her eyes.

"Flip her over," Benjamin instructed. He was applying the flame to something metal, but she couldn't make out exactly what it was.

A seal maybe? A piece of jewelry?

Anne felt her body being turned. She didn't resist.

A moment later, footsteps approached.

"You think—"

"She's my property now, Jessie. I will leave my mark to let everyone know how she cuckolded me."

"Are you—?"

"Shut up, Jessie. Just shut the fuck up."

There was a pause, and then she felt a tingling sensation on her back, just above her left butt cheek. Under normal circumstances, she would have screamed, thrashed, called out. But this *wasn't* normal; nothing about any of this, about feeding Veronica her breast milk or being raped by Benjamin and Jessie, was *normal*.

Even when she smelled her own burning flesh, she failed to react.

There was more laughter, and then the footsteps slowly faded away.

For some reason, the only thought that entered Anne's mind then was that she couldn't remember seeing the doll, seeing Mother, as Terry called her, on the ground where her daughter had dropped it when Jane had burst through the door.

Jane took it. Or maybe Benjamin.

Anne LaForet lay in complete darkness for a long time before finally passing out.

Chapter 16

Time heals all wounds.

Wallace had said that, or at least Anne thought he had.

It wasn't true, of course. The pain that Jane and her husband and Jessie had inflicted on her that night would stay with her until her dying day.

Time *numbed* all wounds, was probably more accurate.

The whip marks on Anne's face, back, and arm all left scars, the worst being the inch-thick gash on her cheek. Still, she was glad to be alive; glad that they had left her slumped, broken, but alive.

And they had either decided to leave Teresa alone or they hadn't known that she was home at the time; it didn't matter which. What mattered was that both she and Terry were still alive.

Anne stayed inside for the week following the incident, allowing Terry to help her nurse her wounds. The girl didn't ask many questions, for which Anne was grateful. She hoped deep down that her daughter had somehow fallen asleep and hadn't seen or heard what had happened.

Somehow, though, especially given the particularly vacant look in Terry's eyes, Anne didn't think that this was the case.

Time numbs all wounds.

"Are we going to be okay, Mommy?" Terry asked, in one of the brief interludes of very few words exchanged during that first week.

Anne couldn't lie to her daughter.

"I don't know, Terry. I don't know."

And that was the truth.

Take your money and leave this place... the people of the swamp never forget.

Anne didn't need the old woman in the market to tell her that she should get out of the swamp, take Terry and just run. But that was pretty much where the fantasy ended.

Where would they go? They didn't have as much money as Anne had initially thought, and even if they had a place to go, hitching a ride would prove difficult. Not many horses in the swamp were for hire, and even if they were, Anne had the sneaking suspicion that the people of the swamp would be less than eager to help her out.

She should have been smarter. She should have saved more.

But there had just been no way of knowing that things would take such a turn...

On the second week after the encounter, a woman from the swamp, one that Anne recognized, came to visit. She was young, barely twenty, and wanted a child.

Anne turned her away.

Two other women came shortly thereafter, but Anne's response was the same as it had been for the previous.

When the fourth woman came, Anne completely lost it and screamed in her face.

"Leave me alone!"

And the woman had. Either her reaction or her scars kept the others away. For a time, as their dwindling produce stocks reduced to nothing, things went back to the way they had been *before*. And Anne slowly came to grips with this fact. All of her fleeting wealth and prosperity was behind her, but this didn't bother her as much as she had thought it might. She had Terry, and that was enough.

Still, things would never be completely normal again, she knew. *Never*.

When the fresh food supplies exhausted, Anne and her daughter went back to choking down dry oats. Her nipples, particularly the left, were horribly disfigured, which made even the thought of expressing her milk enough to cause her entire body to seize. By the time Anne finally considered this option, her supply had all dried up. She doubted that she would have been able to breastfeed ever again, for her own child or for others.

No one asked her what had happened to her face. Things went back to the way they had been right after Wallace had passed. The people of the swamp started to take a wide berth around her at the market, issuing their sidelong glances filled with pity. Even the women that she'd helped bring children into this world treated her as if they had never met.

Anne was worse than a widow to them. Now she was a damaged widow, a strange widow with scars on her face and body. She had become something that the people of the swamp couldn't possibly understand.

But for Anne and Teresa, it was as close to normal as it was going to get.

That is, until Jane returned.

Chapter 17

Anne froze—it was as if her entire body was suddenly encased in ice. She simply couldn't move.

The knock wasn't like the other women from the swamp—tentative, uncertain—or like when Jane had come the last time—deep, loud bangs. Instead, it was the same knock that Anne had heard what seemed like an eon ago. Slow and light, as if the person's knuckles were simply grazing the wood.

It was Jane; there was no question about it. Even though Terry was already asleep, Anne's eyes immediately went into the bedroom door, her thoughts turning to her daughter.

They came back for her—Jane couldn't get pregnant, so she came for Teresa. To take her.

It seemed ridiculous, but given what Mr. and Mrs. Heath had done to Anne, she thought that no matter how farfetched, it was a real possibility.

The knock came again as Anne sat like a statue at the kitchen table, unable to decide what course of action she should take.

Run? Hide?

But Anne did neither of these.

She couldn't; she couldn't do anything.

Rooted in place, Anne's eyes flicked to the door next. After what had happened, she had not only gotten into the habit of locking the door, but she had installed a wooden brace as further security at night.

"Anne? Anne, you in there?" Jane's voice was quiet, meek. Just as it had been three months ago.

A trick—it's a trick. She wants Teresa—she's trying to trick you into opening the door.

"Anne?"

For some reason, this mention of her name snapped the frost off Anne, and she found herself finally able to move again. Part of her was amazed that she managed to remain so calm, that her heart rate had only raised a little bit, and the only sweat that broke out on her skin was on her palms.

But part of her also knew that time numbed all wounds and that there was only so much that Jane could do to her that hadn't already been done.

But they can take Teresa.

Anne silently slid off her chair and landed on all fours on the floor. It was dusk out, which meant that she hadn't lit the lantern yet.

That was something.

Jane didn't know that she was in there — she might assume that the place was abandoned, that Anne had taken Teresa and fled the swamp, like the old hag in the market had suggested.

But if Jane thinks it's abandoned, she might break in to make sure. She might even come in to see if there is any milk left over, any that I may have forgotten to take with me.

Anne slithered beneath the table, trying to push these scenarios from her mind in an attempt to maintain the strange calmness that washed over her.

"Anne? I wanted to come by, tell you that I'm sorry. I — I just lost control, I didn't mean to — to — shit, I can't believe what I did to you."

Anne stared at the front door from beneath the kitchen table. It was hard to comprehend after what had happened that just three months ago she had been sitting across from the woman that was now outside, planning her future with Teresa.

And now the woman sounded much like she had back then, and not like the crazed lady with the horse whip.

A trick—it's a trick.

Anne waited in silence, her eyes flicking from the front door to see if it opened, to Teresa's room for the same reason. If either of them opened, she would be forced to act.

Anne just wasn't sure what she would do in either case.

For a brief moment, Anne was transported back to another time, back before the accident at the Mill. Anne, Wallace, and Teresa had been at the edge of the swamp, all three of them with identical smiles on their faces, their lower bodies caked with mud.

"You see that log there?" Wallace said, pointing at a particularly gnarled piece of driftwood about twenty feet from the shoreline.

Anne nodded, and Teresa said, "Yeah."

"Well, what if I were to tell you that that's the same log I saw when I was here with my dad more than twenty years ago?"

Teresa seemed to mull this over, her eyes scanning the vast swamp before them.

"No way, Daddy."

"Yeah," Anne chimed in. "No way."

They all giggled.

"How can you know it's the same log?"

Wallace smirked, his smile breaking the thick black beard that covered his face. He bent down and picked up a stick.

"Because," he said with a grunt as he launched the branch toward the log, "that's not a log."

The stick landed within a foot of the "log," splashing water several feet in the air. To Anne and Teresa's surprise, the log moved—it actually *moved.*

Anne took a step backward, confused. But then the log moved again, and two yellow reptilian eyes raised out of the swamp.

Anne stumbled, slipping and falling to the mud. She was still holding little Teresa's hand, barely two years old, and she pulled the girl down with her.

Wallace laughed.

"That's not a log," he said, the smirk still plastered on his face. "That's old Ghengis, a gator that's as old as the swamp itself."

"Wally!" Anne shouted. "What about Teresa!"

Ghengis opened his mouth, revealing so many long yellow teeth that Anne couldn't even contemplate counting them all. Teresa would have fit inside that gaping maw with no problem — five Teresas would have fit in there.

Wallace turned and scooped both his wife and daughter out of the mud in a giant bear hug.

"Don't worry," he said, his eyes glittering in the moonlight. "He's old and crusty, but friendly enough. Besides, nothing's going to happen to you guys. At least not while I'm around."

Anne swallowed hard.

But you aren't around anymore, are you, Wallace?

"Anne, I don't know what came over me. I was just—just—well, I guess you know." Her voice dropped an octave. "Benjamin stopped hitting me, at least for now."

There was another long pause, during which Anne held her breath.

"I don't know if you care—I don't blame you if you don't. I wanted to give you something, Anne. But I want to give it to you in person. I'll come back. Next month, I'll come back. I'm just so sorry."

Footsteps receded away from the house, but Anne didn't move. Tears streamed down her face and her back started to ache, but she remained glued to the floor beneath her kitchen table nonetheless.

Only after the moon had reached its apex in the sky did she dare move. But Anne's first inclination wasn't to rise. Instead, her hand instinctively went to the scar on her back. Not the one made by Jane's whip, but the one made by what she now knew was Benjamin's ring that he had heated with the box of matches.

The one that had branded her with his initials. With *BH*.

Where are you now, Wallace? Why aren't you protecting us now when we really need it?

Chapter 18

"No, no, no..." The words came tumbling out of Anne's mouth in such rapid succession that they soon melded into one unintelligible moan. Sobs racked her entire body, and she clutched her stomach as she stood alone in the bathroom.

"Please, no..."

Her mind was a tortured mess, unable to form any rational thought. The only thing that stopped the word *no* from spewing from between her pale lips was another lurch of nausea. Her guts roiled, an undulation that made its way slowly upward, serpentine-like, until it hit her throat.

Anne gagged and then vomited a thin gruel that consisted of nothing but bile and partially digested oats. With spit and puke trailing from her mouth, she said the word again.

"No."

A voice from outside the bathroom door made Anne's eyes bulge and her heart race.

"Mommy? You okay?"

Teresa; it's only Teresa.

Gasping, trying to force the sobs and the rest of her breakfast, lunch, and dinner back down to the dark, infinite pit that was her stomach, Anne somehow managed to formulate an intelligible sentence.

"Fine, sweetie, go play with the—" Another uncontrollable wave of nausea struck her, and she was helpless to prevent it from taking over her entire being. Her stomach flexed, her hands biting into the hard side of the metal basin with such strength that the muscles in her arms started to burn.

More puke came.

"Mom? Mom!"

On the verge of hyperventilating, Anne struggled to get the words out.

"Fine, just—just not feeling *weeeeell*."

The final word was drawn out as she puked again.

"Mom!"

"Fine," she gasped. "Fine, just sick. Please, just *go*."

Anne couldn't believe it. It just wasn't *possible*.

As her nausea passed, she managed to slowly rise into some semblance of standing.

She stared at her reflection in the mirror. Her skin was so pale that it bordered on translucent. Her face was thin, gaunt, her eyes sunken and rimmed with black charcoal. Her lips were pale, her hair a matted mess atop her head. The nipple on her left breast was a mangled mess, just a dark smear, while the right was more defined, but ragged, as if it had been chewed on by a mangy dog.

Despite her thin arms and legs, her stomach held a little weight, the area just above the dark thatch of pubic hair thicker, swollen.

"No."

She turned ever so slightly, intending to view the pouch in her lower abdomen from the side. Instead, she caught a glimpse of the two letters, raised scars that while normally pink, now almost seemed to glow.

BH.

Anne's mind was transported elsewhere, to another time.

Benjamin Heath was on top of her, him being so tall that his narrow chest was in her face, and with each thrust of his hips, his clavicle struck her in the chin, driving the back of her head into the floor.

"*Now I know why Jane liked you so much... now I know why Jane wanted you so much...*"

Anne was sobbing again, tears streaming down her face.

Wallace, where are you? Why did you leave us?

Somewhere in the back of her mind, she realized that there was someone outside the bathroom door again.

"Mom? What's going on in there?"

"I'm—I'm just sick, honey," Anne lied, still staring at her own reflection.

I'm sick, honey... and you're going to be a big sister.

Chapter 19

"Anne? Anne, it's me, Jane. I brought you something—some money. I brought you some money. I'm going to leave it here, on the doorstep. I'm going to leave it here and leave you alone. I won't come back; I won't bother you anymore. Okay? Please, just let me know that you are okay."

Teresa squeezed her hand so hard that Anne was inclined to look at her daughter despite how badly she wanted to hang her head over the basin and vomit some more. For the life of her, Anne couldn't remember if she had felt this sick while pregnant with Teresa.

For some reason, though, she thought not.

"Shh," Anne whispered. "Don't say a word."

They sat in the darkness for at least a minute. It was near midnight, Anne supposed, although her only indication of the time was the fact that it was pitch black in the entire house. Sometime during the middle of the night, she had awoken with a curdled stomach, and despite her best efforts to remain quiet, Terry had felt her rise from the bed.

"Anne?"

Terry squeezed her hand again and Anne squeezed back.

Teresa didn't *know* any of what had happened, and although she was smart enough to know that Anne was pregnant, that was the extent of her understanding. If Anne had any say in the matter, the girl would never know the truth.

"Don't say a word," Anne repeated in a whisper so quiet that she could barely hear the words inside her own head. A sudden wave of nausea passed over her, but Anne gulped it away.

"Please, Anne, I am going to leave now, I just need to see you..."

This time, Anne couldn't help but vomit. She tried her best to do it as quietly as possible, but it was no use. Her vomiting was violent and a full-body affair.

"Anne!"

Hidden in the bathroom, both Terry and Anne heard the front door suddenly burst open.

I forgot to lock it. I forgot to lock it. I forgot to lock it.

"No," Anne muttered.

But it was too late.

Jane was inside, and a moment later, the woman was at the bathroom door. Anne ushered Terry behind her crouched body protectively. As the door to the bathroom was slowly eased open, Anne tried to straighten, to rise to her feet to meet the woman, but she couldn't. It felt as if someone had driven an iron spike through her guts and was turning and twisting it, causing pain and contractions with every rotation.

Jane stood in the doorway for a moment, her eyes flicking from Anne to Terry and back again, an expression of pure confusion on her face. Then she stepped into action, leaning down on one knee and gently laying a hand on Anne's back.

Relief washed over Anne as she realized that this wasn't a trick after all, and that Jane really was here to apologize. But this sensation was quickly overshadowed by the urge to vomit again. As she puked into the basin, she felt Jane's hand gently stroke her back.

"What's wrong? Are you ill? Did you eat something sour?"

Anne shook her head. Her blonde hair, damp with sweat, the ends soaked in vomit, whipped back and forth, before clinging to her cheeks. Jane reached out and eased her hair back, pulling it from the basin. Somehow Anne managed to shift to a sitting position, the twisting in her guts abating for the moment.

"Thank you," she said, wiping her mouth with the back of her hand.

Jane stood.

"You're welcome. Are you sure you aren't ill? Do you need a doctor?"

Again, Anne shook her head, but this time she couldn't maintain eye contact.

"Well," Jane began, "I came to say that I am sorry. I know that nothing I can say can take back what I said or what I did, but—"

The woman hesitated and her eyes narrowed as she tried to make sense of the scene before her. While it was clear that her apology had been rehearsed, finding Anne in the bathroom in her present state clearly hadn't been part of the script. As Jane's eyes scanned her body, Anne grew uncomfortable and she instinctively pulled her shirt over the small bump below her belly button.

This was a mistake.

Despite how subtle she had been, Jane caught this gesture and her eyes grew wide. In a split second, any semblance of compassion or guilt left the woman's face and it contorted into something else. Her nostrils flared, her nose scrunched, and her lips pressed together so tightly that they quickly lost any of their natural pink hue.

It was the same expression that Anne had seen the night when Jane had accosted her with the horse whip.

"You're pregnant," Jane sneered. Her hands fell to her sides, but this wasn't a defenseless gesture. Instead, they formed fists, and although they were nowhere near the size of her husband's, they were more pointed and jagged.

Dangerous.

"No," Anne said. She instinctively shuffled her body in front of Terry, who was breathing heavily behind her. This time, there was no chance for Anne to send her daughter to her room; the doorway was completely blocked by Jane Heath's tense body.

"You're *fucking* pregnant. After all this, *you* get pregnant. After all I have been through." She took a step forward. "You already have a fucking kid, you ungrateful swamp whore."

"Don't hurt her," Terry whimpered.

The little girl's words went ignored.

"You shouldn't have gone and done that, Anne. You shouldn't have gotten yourself pregnant. That wasn't *right*."

Still seated, Anne pushed herself backward with her hands, forcing Terry back with her. It was the best she could do; shrouding her child with her own body was her only chance of protecting her. Whatever punishment that was about to be inflicted on her, she could take it, deal with it.

She was numb.

But not Terry.

For some reason, she was struck by the realization that Teresa's fourth birthday was only a few days away.

Please don't hurt Terry—she's just a little girl. She's innocent, she had nothing to do with any of this.

Jane lowered herself onto her haunches to stare Anne directly in the face.

There was hatred in Jane's blue irises. Hatred born out of years of abuse at the hands of her husband, at years of being punched and kicked and too scared to either strike back or even to run.

But now... now Jane could do anything she wanted. Jane could seek revenge on all those who had ever hurt her.

Her fists unballed, and her lips turned into a patronizing frown.

"Oh, what, are you scared, swamp peasant?" she asked in a childish voice. Anne cringed and squeezed her eyes closed as Jane's hand shot out. To her surprise, it didn't slap or scratch her or even strike her as Anne had expected. Instead, it gently caressed her cheek. "Open your eyes."

Anne obliged.

All she saw was floating white teeth, gapped where there were several of them missing, locked in a mocking smile. Jane's hand slowly moved from her cheek to the back of her head, the fingers intertwining between the wet strands as they tightened.

Anne cried out, but Teresa was the one who acted. The girl grabbed Jane's forearm, her tiny crescent nails biting into her pale skin.

"Don't hurt Mommy!" she shouted, to which Jane responded with a hiss. With her other hand, Jane lashed out, driving her fist into the girl's chest, forcing the air from her lungs and sending her careening backward.

"*No!*" Anne shouted, but the grip on her hair tightened and she found herself unable to rise.

Terry gulped as she stumbled backward, her eyes wide. It looked as if she might continue in this way *ad infinitum*, but then her back struck the wall with a sickening thud. Her eyes rolled back as her body slid down the wall seemingly in slow motion, until she rested on the bathroom floor, slumped and unconscious.

"*No!*" Anne shouted again, tears streaming down her face.

"Stand up, you slut," Jane ordered. The woman stood first, yanking Anne's hair, forcing her to rise as well.

An unexpected pang in her stomach made Anne's legs shoot out and she almost fell back to the ground. She would have fallen if it were not for the impossibly strong grip on her hair. Her left foot struck the basin full of vomit, knocking it onto its side. Anne watched in horror as the thick liquid splashed to the floor, before making a slow, winding course toward Terry's unconscious body. The girl's pants, new ones, ones that Anne had spent the last of her money on, began to turn dark as they soaked up the puke.

"You're lucky I don't kill you," Jane said. Her voice was strange, deeper than Anne remembered. When she looked at the woman, she seemed to have changed.

It wasn't Jane anymore, but Benjamin Heath. Benjamin on top of her, grunting, his hands squeezing her blood-streaked breasts.

"You're lucky," the voice repeated.

And then Jane pulled with the hand tangled in her hair and pivoted at the same time, flinging Anne with all of her strength. Anne swiveled on her heels and tried to root herself, but before she could react, she was flying toward the open bathroom door.

Jane refused to let go of her hair.

Anne flew feet first, and when it was her head's turn to follow the rest of her body, she felt a sharp pain and then sweet release as her hair and part of her scalp peeled away.

Hot liquid immediately soaked the back of her neck.

And then Anne really was completely airborne.

She tried to twist in the air to avoid the narrow door frame, but her efforts were futile. Her right shoulder struck the frame, and she heard a loud crack that was too thick and organic to be the wood. This contact sent her spinning in the air, until she eventually landed on her stomach in the middle of the kitchen, the air forced out of her lungs in an audible *whoosh*.

For a moment, time seemed to stop. Darkness threatened to overwhelm Anne, but she forced it away.

No, not while Terry is still here.

She hoped that it was over. That the damage had been done, that Jane would leave, and that this was the last time she would ever see her.

But a sound, a roar of sheer fury, filled her modest house and she knew that this wasn't the case.

"*You fucking slut!*"

Jane stomped toward Anne, but even raising her head and twisting it around proved difficult. Blood was streaming down her back now, and her shoulder throbbed with intense pain.

"You fucked him? You fucked *him!*"

Anne wasn't sure what the woman with the blazing eyes meant, but she didn't care. All she cared about was making sure that Terry was safe.

Jane was beside her again, crouching down.

She was smiling a wild smile.

In one smooth motion, Jane pulled the sleeve of her dark dress up, showing Anne her forearm. Her arm was so close to Anne's face that, at first, she had a hard time focusing.

And then she saw it and her heart sunk.

On Jane's forearm were two thick pink scars. Ones she recognized.

BH.

When she had been thrown into the kitchen, her shirt must have teased up at the back, showing Jane her matching scars.

"I don't know how you did it, but you fucked him—I know it, because he branded you as his own. I came to you for your help, but you tricked me. You *fucking* tricked me and you stole him from me. You stole him *and* my child."

Anne barely felt the woman's hands on the back of her head this time, her scalp so tacky with blood as it was. The fact that her head was lifted off the wooden floor barely registered.

"I don't know how you fucking did it, but I'll be back for you."

Jane leaned in close and whispered in her ear. Her breath was hot and sour, like warm milk.

"I'll be back for you, *witch*."

It was the last word Anne LaForet heard before the floor rushed up to meet her.

Her mouth hit the hardwood, her front teeth snapping and falling inward, her lips splitting wide from her lower teeth.

And then the darkness that she had so desperately tried to resist, for Terry's sake, was all-encompassing.

Chapter 20

Anne awoke to one single thought: pain.

Every single bone in her body seemed to be either bruised or broken. Blood filled her nose and mouth, and she had to snort and hawk a large glob onto the floor to take a full breath. Despite the darkness of her house, she could still make out several large flecks of white in her bloody spit. She knew that her teeth were smashed, and a cursory probing of her tongue proved as much. Both front teeth were gone, and the teeth on either side were at most half their normal length.

Her head throbbed from the crown all the way down to her hairline at the back of her neck. Remembering the way that the tension had released as her hair and scalp peeled back caused her to shudder.

Blood; she had lost a lot of blood.

Rivers of it filled her mind, and she imagined it leaking from her every pore, winding like snakes across the floor, until it was soaked up by—

Teresa!

An image of her daughter, slumped, unconscious, ignited another flash of pain.

Anne tried to roll from her stomach onto her right side, but she found herself unable to lift or even move that arm. A sliver of moonlight spilled in from the kitchen window as a large cloud rolled by, and she afforded herself a quick look at the damage that Jane had inflicted, if for no other reason but to figure out the best way to make it to her daughter.

Her shoulder was pushed backward at an awkward angle, the joint so far behind her that she couldn't see all of it. Anne knew little of how her body worked, how her bones and muscles operated in concert to allow her to move, but she knew enough to know that her shoulder was completely broken.

Shattered, even.

With a groan, she turned her head to the other side, feeling an uncomfortable squishing sensation as the congealed blood on the back of her neck twisted and chaffed.

"Careful, Mom."

It was Teresa's voice, and Anne hesitated.

"*Shhweetie*? That you?" she asked in a lispy, wet whisper that she didn't recognize as her own.

Anne turned her head all the way, and what she saw answered her own question.

Despite all that had happened, she felt her mouth forming a toothless smile.

Teresa was sitting cross-legged, wearing nothing but a shirt and cotton underwear, staring down at her. The girl had taken a cloth from the kitchen and, judging by the bloodstain on the corner, she had been doing her best to clean Anne up.

It was a losing battle. There was so much blood from Anne's torn scalp alone that it would take more than a cloth, or even ten, to clean it all.

Terry's eyes were red; she had been crying. But to Anne, she looked like the most beautiful thing in the world.

She looked like an angel.

Then reality took over, and questions flooded her mind.

How long has she been sitting there? How long have I been out?

Judging by the dark night sky, it couldn't have been more than four or five hours at most; if it was the same night, of course, which was something that she couldn't count on.

The good news was that Jane was gone again, and they were alone.

"I didn't think you were ever going to wake up, Mommy," Terry sobbed.

Anne grunted and groaned as she turned onto her left side and tried to push herself to her feet. Her first attempt failed.

"I'm here," Anne said, spraying blood from her split lips with every word. "I'm awake."

On her second try, she managed to bring herself to a seated position. The effort made her head spin and stars flash before her eyes.

I've lost a lot of blood.

In addition to a splitting headache, she realized that there was also a strange tightness to her head, as if someone had pumped air into her ear, filling her skull with it like some sort of organic balloon.

"Don't try to stand, Mommy."

Anne started to shake her head, but based on how the pain behind her eyes exploded with just the subtlest of movements, she decided against it.

I'll be back, witch.

"We *musht* go, Terry. We *musht*."

The sound of Anne's own voice made her cry. Despite what she had felt and what she had seen, she had a hard time contemplating how much damage had been inflicted on her body.

But one thing was certain; it was too much, far too much. Maybe even more than what Benjamin and his disgusting henchman had—

The baby!

Anne's hand went to her stomach, rubbing the extra skin there. There was no way of knowing if it was still alive in there. She moved her hand to between her legs, lifting up her skirt and lightly touching her underwear. They came back red.

Part of her wanted to cry, while another part was relieved. She didn't want to bring another baby into her world, especially not one that was the product of rape... that was part Benjamin Heath.

But it was still a baby, and it was a part her, too.

And that made her sad.

"Mom?" Terry said. "Where do we go?"

I'll be back, witch.

Anne somehow managed to ignore the pain for long enough to scramble from a seated position to hunching over on her knees. It didn't matter how long she had been out, Anne realized; it only mattered that they get out of here as quickly as possible. She remembered how Jane's eyes had blazed, how much hatred had been buried deep within those blue eyes. And she remembered the words of the strange woman in the swamp, the ones that had predicted that something like this was inevitable.

"Anywhere," Anne whispered. "Anywhere but the swamp."

Together they shuffled across the floor toward the bedroom door. As they passed beneath the window, Anne couldn't help but straighten her hunched form and take a peek outside.

A modicum of relief struck her when she saw the dark swamp and no horse and carriage. But this feeling was fleeting. She had learned her lesson; she wasn't going to wait around this time for Jane to return.

Anne pulled Terry into the bedroom with her.

"Fill one of the *bagth* with *thum clotheth*; *thum* underwear, a *thirt* and a pair of *thorts*," Anne instructed.

Terry looked confused, but moved to grab one of the bags from beneath the bed.

"Dresses?"

Anne started to shake her head again, but the pain almost sent her crashing to the ground. Her head was just so *tight*. Rational thought was becoming increasingly difficult.

"No, no *dretheth*. Be quick—we need to leave now."

Terry's expression turned serious, and she poked her tongue into her cheek like she always did when she was concentrating. Anne watched as she retrieved the bag, before she turned and headed for the dresser. She yanked open the top drawer and grabbed the small bag of money from inside, which suddenly felt very light in her hand.

Should have saved more, shouldn't have spent so much damn money.

Anne hooked the thin drawstring around her limp right wrist and then turned back to Terry.

"Tereshhha? You—"

A flicker of light caught her eye, and Anne immediately stopped speaking. Their small bedroom only had one window, a perfect square just above the bed. But when Anne peered out through it, she only saw blackness.

She waited as Teresa stared at her, mimicking her mother's frozen posture.

There.

Anne saw it again, a shimmer of light somewhere deep in the swamp. A torch. And as her eyes focused on that torch, she caught a glimpse of another. And then another.

As she watched in horror, her disfigured mouth going slack, she realized that the torches were actually becoming larger and more distinct. They were coming toward the house.

"Tereshhha! Get over here!"

Terry, seeing the expression on her mother's face, dropped the bag that was half stuffed with her clothes and hurried to her side.

Anne knew that her daughter was begging to be held, but she couldn't seem to draw her attention away from the window. In addition to the dots of light coming from deep within the swamp, there was something else about the whole scene that was off.

It took a moment before Anne realized that in addition to the typical swamp noises, she heard another, deeper, more rhythmic sound.

They were chanting.

Whoever was out there with the torches coming toward her house, toward Anne and Teresa LaForet, were *chanting*.

What the fuck?

The people were still too distant for Anne to make out the exact words.

"Let's get out of here, *Tereshhha*," she said again, wrapping her left arm protectively around her daughter. Together they moved out of the bedroom toward the kitchen. Anne had no idea where they would go once outside, but the swamp was vast enough for her and Teresa to hide in it for a very long time, if need be.

Something told her that if she didn't leave now, she never would.

They were halfway to the door when a shout from outside stopped them both cold. Terry started to tremble, which rubbed off on Anne as she slowly raised her eyes to the window.

The moonlight illuminated a figure from behind, brightly outlining her thin frame that was clutching a large, burning torch. Behind her was a horse and carriage that Anne immediately recognized.

Jane had returned, and if her voice was any indication, the anger and hatred that had driven the woman to smash Anne's face into the floor and to knock Teresa unconscious hadn't faded in the least.

"Anne LaForet, I demand that you come out of your home. In the name of the Lord, I command you. Witches are not welcome in the swamp. Come out, and bring your daughter with you."

I'm not a witch, Anne wanted to scream back at the top of her lungs. *Leave me and my daughter alone!*

But she knew she would only be wasting her breath.

The door to her house was off to the side, while Jane, and now several other people brandishing torches, were standing directly in front of the house. Clearly, they expected to frighten her enough to just come outside—to give herself up.

If we can just—

The window that Anne was peering through suddenly smashed inward and she screamed. Teresa also cried out, and Anne instinctively hugged her even harder.

Something solid thumped on the floor, which, in addition to the growing number of burning torches assembling outside her home, spurred Anne to action. But instead of darting toward the door, she crouched and dragged both herself and Teresa beneath the table.

It was her safe place, the place where she had curled up night after night following Wallace's death.

"Come out, you fucking *witch*!" Jane shouted.

Teresa shuddered in Anne's arms, and for some reason a moment of clarity overcame her.

"I'm sorry, Terry. I'm so, so sorry."

But while Terry's body stopped shaking, the girl didn't respond.

It was only then, in that strange moment of calmness, that Anne realized what the people of the swamp were chanting.

Anne knew then, if she hadn't before, that she was doomed. Nothing she could say or do would get her out of this unscathed.

"Burn the witches! Burn the witches!"

She squeezed Teresa's head against her chest, trying to cover both her ears with one hand.

They weren't saying witch, but *witches*.

And Teresa was the only other person here.

"Look," Teresa whispered, pointing at the object that had been thrown through the window. Anne had expected to see a rock or maybe a piece of wood.

But it was neither.

The pale face of the doll she had bought Terry was lying on its back just a few feet from where they huddled beneath the table. There was no body; the head had been torn from the blue dress, the neck ragged with white cotton stuffing spilling out like entrails.

But it was the eyes that were most disturbing—or at least where the eyes *used* to be. They had been gouged out, leaving only two massive, empty sockets that somehow seemed to stare *into* Anne.

"Look, it's Mother," Teresa said, her tiny voice warbling with fear.

Chapter 21

They stripped Anne naked and paraded her through the swamp. Blood was pouring from between her legs, soaking her inner thighs and dripping onto the tops of her bare feet when she pulled them out of the mud.

Jane had done something to her down there, something with a rusty set of pliers. Anne hadn't been sure if the baby was still alive after she had been thrown onto the kitchen floor, but now she knew it was dead.

Dead and gone.

She had no idea where Teresa was. Her only hope was that the girl had somehow escaped and had fled into the swamp when Jane had broken down the door.

This was what she hoped, but she wasn't *hopeful*.

"Burn the witches, burn the witches, burn the witches."

They all had torches, every last one of them. As Anne walked toward the large tree at the edge of her property line, her final destination, she recognized some of the people brandishing the torches and chanting.

Veronica was there, her thin lips twisted into a cruel smile.

I helped you conceive. I saved your marriage, saved you from Ken.

Anne never said the words, but it was as if Veronica could hear them anyway.

"Burn, witch," she said, the light from her torch reflected off her dark brown irises, making them glow. Then she reared back and propelled forward, spit flying from her mouth.

The gob struck Anne just below her left eye, but she didn't brush it away, didn't even flinch.

Instead, she just kept walking forward.

She passed Christine next and, like Veronica, her mouth was twisted into a sneer.

I helped you too, Christine.

The woman hissed, then reached out with her hand. Again, Anne didn't move, and her lack of reaction caught Christine off guard. Although her hand was initially aimed at her face, she changed trajectory at the last moment and instead her fingers got tangled in the trail of hair and scalp that hung partway down her back.

Feeling that, Christine immediately recoiled.

The other women that she had helped were there too.

One foot in front of the other, Anne continued forward. At some point during her march, she ceased feeling pain or even the mud between her toes. She didn't even feel the first object, a rock, she thought, ricochet off her left hip. She didn't feel the punches or the kicks that the crowd started to deliver, which were small, cautious blows at first, but spurred by her lack of reaction, they became full strikes. Twice Anne was knocked to the ground, but she always rose again, her naked body covered with blood and mud.

She felt *nothing*.

Anne was almost at the small stool, a roughly made piece of wood at the base of the large tree, when she spotted a crooked figure leaning out from behind one of the trees. Unlike the other women, she wasn't chanting, or smiling, or even looking angry. The woman's leathery face was apathetic. Forlorn, even.

Anne didn't know if the woman from the market spoke or just mouthed the words, but they echoed in her head nonetheless.

The people of the swamp never forget.

Anne, for some strange reason, felt herself nodding.

I am from the swamp. I will never forget.

Jane suddenly appeared beside her.

"Yeah, that's right. Up on the stool, witch." Her voice was low and even, cutting through the *burn the witches* mantra that filled the humid swamp air. "*Mater est, matrem omnium.*"

Anne continued forward. When she made it to the stool, she stepped up without hesitation, then turned to face her accusers, pressing her back against the tree.

They were *all* there, she realized. Every single one of the women that she had helped, and everyone else that she had ever known from the swamp. There were the men and women that Wallace had worked with at the Mill, the people that she had sold her wooden scarecrows to what seemed like a year ago.

And all of them had torches in their hands and identical looks on their faces.

"*Burn the witches!*"

Anne felt a rope wrap around her neck, pulling her flush against the tree. And then Jane suddenly appeared before her, her eyes narrowed, her mouth twisted into an evil smirk.

"Bring out the girl."

Anne finally reacted.

"No!" she screamed through her smashed teeth. "No! *No!*"

Anne struggled against the rope, trying to get free, to get at Jane, but it tightened so quickly that she suddenly found it hard to breathe.

"Yes," Jane whispered, nodding vigorously. She held her hands out at her sides, and the crowd silenced. "Bring out the *girl!*" she hollered over her shoulder.

The crowd stirred behind Jane, and a small figure was shoved so hard from behind that she fell into the mud.

Nobody helped her up.

When she raised her head, Anne got the confirmation that she'd been dreading.

It was Teresa.

Jane turned to face the girl.

"Go on, go on up and stand by your mother, *witch*."

Terry's eyes went wide, but she did as she was instructed.

Run, Terry! Run!

But the girl didn't run. Instead, she rose up and hugged Anne. Anne hugged back, both of their bodies hitching with sobs. A second rope was looped around first the tree and then both of their waists, keeping them forever locked in an embrace.

Jane turned her back to Anne and her daughter and addressed the crowd in a loud, booming voice.

"We all know why we are here... we are here to punish the witches that have infiltrated your swamp. You all know what these two have done—they have practiced the dark art of witchcraft in their home."

Jane turned back to Anne and sneered. She looked her directly in her eyes when she shouted her next words.

"And what do we do to witches in the swamp?"

The response was instantaneous and unanimous.

"Burn them!"

Jane nodded.

"That's right, we burn witches in the swamp."

Without warning, the woman reared back and threw her torch at Anne's feet. Anne instinctively held Terry close, but didn't bother trying to lift her feet to avoid the sparks that shot up to greet them.

Jane turned back to the crowd when she was confident that the small platform that Anne and Terry stood on had started to catch fire.

"Anne and Teresa LaForet are witches. And even worse, Anne is *mater est, matrem omnium.*"

Anne had heard the words before, although she couldn't remember where.

They meant, simply, *mother of one, mother of all.*

And, in a way, it seemed oddly appropriate.

"Burn your effigies beneath her feet to cleanse yourself of the wicked workings of these witches."

There was a slight hesitation, but then a woman—Kyra, Anne thought—stepped forward and threw one of the wooden scarecrow figurines into the fire beneath her feet. Anne had traded it to her in the market for a handful of rice. Back then, Kyra had smiled at her, her eyes filled with pity.

There was no pity in those eyes now.

Another woman came next, one that Anne didn't recognize, and she tossed her scarecrow at the fire as well.

Anne's feet started to burn, and Terry started to shift from one foot to another.

The townspeople came fast and furious next, each and every one of them tossing more wooden figurines beneath her feet. There were so many of the damn things that Anne was taken aback.

Did I make all of those?

For some reason, instead of contemplating this, Anne turned her head skyward. The moon had reached its apex, the glowing ball shining down on both her and her daughter.

It was past midnight, she figured. Which meant that it was Terry's birthday. She had just turned four.

Sadness overcame her then, and she lowered her mangled lips to the top of Terry's head, straining against the ropes to do so.

She kissed her daughter.

"I'm sorry, Terry. I'm sorry, sweetie. I'm so sorry."

The girl said nothing, but she stopped shifting.

The flames were higher now, and when Anne turned her head forward, she locked eyes with Jane.

"Burn the witches!" she shouted. "*Filia obcisor, filius obcisor.*"

And for some reason, Anne knew those words, too.

Daughter killer, son killer.

"*Mater est, matrem omnium.*"

The fire was getting too big, too hot, and Jane was forced to take a step backward. She repeated the three phrases, and once again the crowd joined in with her.

It became a new chant.

This time, however, Anne wasn't frightened into silence. Instead, she laughed.

Jane's smile faded.

"You said you would come back for me," Anne said. "But now let me tell you the same. *I* will come back for *you.*"

Then Anne LaForet closed her eyes and the flames engulfed both her and her daughter.

Chapter 22

The fire finally stopped burning in the early dawn.

Anne was gone. Teresa was gone. At some point throughout the night, the townsfolk had left as well, receding back to their homes and lives as if nothing had happened. As if they had done a good thing, ridding this world of two witches.

They had taken their chants with them.

Only Jane Heath remained, her eyes still locked on the smoldering rubble. Several bones were clearly visible in the ashes — those needed much higher heat to melt away. But any of what had made Anne or Teresa LaForet human, their skin and hair and muscle, had long since been reduced to ash.

"Fucking witch," Jane said as she leaned over the larger of the two gleaming skulls. She spat on the skull, but it still wasn't enough for her — this sacrilege, this utter desecration of the dead, simply wasn't enough to satisfy her need for revenge.

Not for Jane Heath, wife to Benjamin Heath, co-owner of the largest plantation in Charleston. Anne LaForet deserved worse; she deserved more than being burned alive at the stake, still embracing her daughter.

After all, she had used witchcraft to seduce her husband, after first coercing Jane into revealing her secrets. And that was only the start; then she had gone and become pregnant with Benjamin's seed, housing the bastard child in her belly. A child that should have been *her* child.

Jane took a large step toward the gleaming bones, swatting away some of the larger flies that buzzed about in the already warm morning air. She had to take wide steps on either side of the pile of bones and black tar-like substance to avoid burning her feet. The fire might have burnt out, but the remains were still hot, making the air above them hazy with heat.

But this didn't deter Jane.

Spreading her feet as widely as possible, she stepped over the pile and then squatted.

The air was hot on the bare skin between her legs, and it took a few seconds for her to get comfortable. But eventually she did, and with a soft moan, a thin stream of urine splashed from beneath her dress and onto the pile of bones. It hissed like an angered snake when it landed.

Jane smirked.

Witches got what they deserved.

She shook, then started to stand when something across the lawn on the edge of the property line caught her eye.

There was a person hiding behind one of the trees. Squinting hard, she could make out a woman—a hunched woman, old and decrepit—leaning out from behind one of the tree trunks. Her patchy hair was long and gray, hanging in front of her face. The shadows made it impossible to see her eyes, but she made out a crooked nose and a nearly lipless mouth.

What the fuck?

The woman's mouth started to widen into a smile. A large, toothless grin.

"Hey!" Jane shouted, shaking the last of her pee. "Hey, what are you doing? *Hey!*"

But the woman's mouth kept getting wider and wider, until it stretched well beyond normal limits. The sight made Jane's stomach flip. When the gaping orifice seemed to encompass her entire face, she couldn't take it anymore and looked away.

Jesus—

She went to stand, suddenly overcome by a sense of dread.

Only she couldn't.

"What the—?"

Jane tried to lift her feet again, to stop squatting and get away from Anne and Teresa LaForet's remains, but her feet seemed rooted. A gasp escaped her and she frantically yanked her dress up higher, looking around the sides of the dark blue fabric to see beneath her—to see what sort of strange mud had encased her feet. But it wasn't mud that held her in place.

"Oh my God," she moaned.

The earth beneath Jane seemed to have split, a glowing two-inch gash running directly through the center of the smoldering ashes. And out of that fissure arose a thick black gas, but it wasn't like the smog or smoke she occasionally noticed from chimneys back in Charleston.

This was different. The smoke was tight and controlled, and it seemed not to move through the air at the whim of the breeze, but instead, it migrated with purpose. The smoke probed her undercarriage, pushing up against the sensitive skin between her legs.

Her heart beating in triple-time, Jane cried out and she again tried to lift her legs and flee this place—to leave the swamp once and for all. But it was too late. Whatever had seeped out of the split in the ground and gripped her wasn't letting go. Without warning, the dark cloud drove *into* her.

Jane's head was thrown back, her eyes rolling backward, her mouth opening nearly as wide as that of the old hag in the swamp. A croak exited her throat as her body was racked with a tremor that lasted for an eternity.

And throughout it all, Jane heard one phrase repeated over and over and over again.

I told you I would come back.

I—told—you—I—would—come—back.

EPILOGUE

"You really think she came back here, Ben?"

Benjamin Heath pulled his horse to a stop just in front of the modest wood house. It looked much different in the day—more rundown, dilapidated.

Sad.

He paused, sniffing the air. It smelled faintly of barbecue.

A small gust of wind swayed the porch swing, causing the chain to squeak, drawing Benjamin's attention back.

"Yeah, the bitch is here somewhere. I'll find her."

Both men dismounted. They went into the house first, the door of which was slightly ajar. Inside, they found a smashed window and a pile of dried blood in the center of the room. The smell of cooked meat was stronger here, but there was an unsettling funk underlying it all.

Benjamin kicked a doll's head across the room and Jessie whistled.

"What you think happened here?"

Benjamin shushed him.

"Be quiet."

The man obliged.

It was out back on the boggy ground leading to the edge of the swamp that they found Jane's horse. The animal was lying on its side, its neck twisted all the way around. The horse's eyes had been gouged out, the sockets in which they had once lain filled with dried black blood.

"*Fuuuck*," Jessie groaned. "What could have done this?"

The man covered his mouth after he spoke the words, clearly worried that they would be promptly followed by vomit. Ben shot him a look, but Jessie failed to notice. His eyes remained locked on the horse, and when Benjamin strode forward, he did so alone.

When he cleared the side of the house, he saw her. Near the edge of the property, beside a tree with a pile of charred wood or something else—the source of the barbecue smell, perhaps—there was a woman squatting in front of a plain white cross pushed into the mud, her back to him.

Squinting in the midday sun, Benjamin took a hesitant step forward.

Jane? What the fuck are you doing?

It certainly looked like Jane, only her posture, all pointed and crooked angles, was off.

He swallowed hard and took a step toward her, then another. He kept his eyes locked on the woman as he walked, trying to pick up the subtle rise and fall of her back. He didn't see any. In fact, Benjamin didn't see any movement at all from the hunched, squatted figure.

A hand came down on his shoulder, and Benjamin leaped in the opposite direction, his heart thumping so loudly in his chest that it was nearly audible. Sweat immediately broke out on his forehead.

"Shit, sorry, Ben." Jessie's eyes were wide, and his lower lip trembling.

Ben shoved the man away, but this had little effect on the terrified man.

"I found Clyde—Jane's carriage driver—fuck, he was just like the horse... eyes all gouged out, head turned around backward. What the *fuck* could have done that?"

Ben didn't hear any of what his friend was saying. Instead, he focused all of his attention on Jane's curled spine. Even with the commotion, he hadn't detected even the slightest movement.

Jessie must have seen her then too, as he suddenly reached out and grabbed Benjamin's upper arm. Ben tried to shake him off, but the man's grip was as strong as his fear was palpable.

When the woman—it was Jane, it had to be Jane—slowly unfurled her back and stood, both men held their collective breaths. She turned and when she finally faced them, Benjamin let out a sigh of relief; he didn't even care if Jessie heard it.

It *was* Jane.

"Jane," he said, but then he remembered why he was here, and he lowered his voice a few octaves. "What the fuck are—?"

"Jane?" the woman asked, her manicured eyebrows rising high up her forehead.

Benjamin swallowed hard.

"What—?"

"No, not Jane," she said with a smile.

"Jane, what the fuck?"

Benjamin shrugged away the confusion and took two aggressive steps forward.

Jane laughed, a tight, high-pitched sound. Then she raised her hand, stopping him cold.

"No, my name's not Jane—it's Mother. You can call me Mother."

Benjamin Heath didn't even notice Jessie's fingernails biting into his forearm so hard that they started to draw blood.

"You can call me *mater est, matrem omnium.*"

END

Author's Note

I hope you enjoyed this prequel to the *Family Values Trilogy*. Of course, this is only the beginning of the tale of Jane Heath and the swamp, of *mater est, matrem omnium*. As the name of the trilogy suggests, at its heart the *Family Values Trilogy* is about just that: family values.

But it's also about murder, possession, kidnapping, fear, horror… you get the idea. If you liked *Witch*, the first book *MOTHER* is going to be right up your alley. To whet your appetite, I have included a preview following this note.

Also be sure to check out my best-selling *Insatiable Series*, which, is about a town trying to survive in the face of unspeakable evil.

To keep up to date on sales and new releases, be sure to like my Facebook page @authorpatricklogan.

Have a glass of warm milk before bed. It'll help you sleep.

Take care,
Patrick
Montreal, 2016

…and now, as promised, for your sneak peek of Book 1 in the *Family Values Trilogy*, **MOTHER**…

Mother
Family Values Trilogy
Book 1

Prologue (Conception)

The girl stared at her reflection in the mirror as the steam from the shower billowed about her soft, pale skin.

She brought a hand to her chest and gently lifted her right breast, assessing the weight of it before allowing gravity to bring it back to its resting place.

It seemed bigger today.

No, not bigger—bigger is the wrong word for it. More full. Definitely more full.

Her nipples, hard despite the moist, warm air that engulfed her body, looked a little darker than usual as well, but she chalked this up to her imagination.

This can't be happening... not yet.

She felt like crying.

While most girls her age might have confused what was happening to her body as part of the transition into adulthood, she knew that *this* was not *that*. Her first blood had come and gone many months earlier—young for her age—and she was smart enough to know that the changes her body was undergoing were happening far too quickly to be puberty-related.

No, *this* was something else entirely.

A deep frown, one that wrinkled the smooth skin around the corners of her lips and caused a rash of unsightly dimples to riddle her round chin, made its way onto her face. The desire to cry, to simply drop to her knees and sob, was nearly overwhelming, and it took all of her willpower to resist.

This, too—controlling her emotions—would become more difficult as her body underwent even further changes. Hormonal changes.

The girl turned sideways, her brow furrowing as she scrutinized her profile in the foggy mirror.

It can't be. Please, don't let it be true.

Her hands moved from her breasts to the spot just below her navel, to the slight but perceptible pouch of skin perfectly situated above the muscles that descended into a '*v*' between her legs.

It couldn't be—but it *was*.

No.

If it hadn't been for her breath catching in her throat, the word would have escaped her lips in a moan. And that would have had disastrous consequences.

As she watched, her reflection began to blur, the edges becoming hazy like headlights cutting through thick fog. It was the condensation from the shower that gave her outline an ethereal quality, which was only fitting as her situation was anything *but* real.

A sound from just outside the bathroom door startled her, and she paused.

"Sweets?"

A split-second hesitation was all it took; such a small, seemingly inconsequential act, but it carried with it severe repercussions. The girl swiveled on her bare heels, spinning so quickly toward the half-open bathroom door that she narrowly avoided pirouetting into the corner of the bone-white vanity. Yet despite her spin, she had acted too slowly.

The neatly folded load of laundry that lay artfully across her mother's arms—a pile of colorful socks, graphic t-shirts, and a couple pairs of jeans—fell to the ground in what seemed like slow motion.

The girl slammed her palm against the bathroom door, closing it with a loud bang.

"Mother!" she shouted, hoping that the anger in her voice usurped the fear—the embarrassment. "Mother! Privacy, please!"

After wiping the tears from her eyes, the girl pressed both hands against the back of the door as if she were preparing for her own 'Here's Johnny' moment.

Or maybe she was waiting for that dreaded knock, or the sound of her mother's patronizing voice.

But there was no sound from her room, which, in a way, was worse.

Say something!

The girl pressed her ear against the door between her hands. Had Mother not seen? She fought the urge to look down at herself.

Is it not that noticeable?

She had slammed the door closed so quickly that she hadn't seen her mother's eyes... instead, she had been distracted by the falling laundry, the striped candy cane socks that had done a little dance as they tumbled to the carpeted bedroom floor.

Could she have been distracted by the laundry as well?

Her mind raced.

Say something! Anything!

Her hopes were dashed when she finally heard her mother's voice, her words coming out low and slow, the universal pitch that mothers used to let their children know that they were serious, that they meant *business*.

Oh, the woman had seen alright—she missed nothing.

"Open the door," her mother ordered.

The girl pressed her forehead against the back of the door and squeezed her eyes shut.

Fuck! How could I have been so stupid?

Tears somehow managed to leak from between her closed lids and made wet tracks down both of her round cheeks. The liquid felt oddly cool on her skin, cutting through the steam that had coated the mirror and saturated the air with what felt like a thick paste. The humid air had begun to settle on all surfaces—including herself.

Hot, sticky, uncomfortable air.

Her heart rate soared.

Please—just leave.

"Open the door."

Please.

When her mother spoke a third time, her voice was different. It wasn't calm and demanding, but tight, bordering on hysterical. The sudden change in pitch shocked the girl into opening her eyes.

"You can't have it! You need to get it out!"

'You need to get it out.' She could barely believe that her mother had uttered those words. *It. Get it out.*

The girl felt as if her soul had been crushed, as if all of her bones had suddenly been turned to dust and she was but a pile of skin lying on the wet bathroom floor.

"It's not—"

—*what you think*, was what she wanted to say, but her mother cut her off.

"You're pregnant," the woman hissed.

Hearing those words out loud, even though she'd known them to be true long before her mother had come into her room carrying her stupid fucking striped socks, somehow made it all real.

I'm just bloated, Mom, she wanted to say. *It's just my stupid period, Mom.*

But the only words that she could manage were, "I'm sorry."

And with the utterance of those two words, so very benign on their own, but when combined carried so much weight, tears began to fall in a deluge.

How did this happen?

Her body hitched against the back of the door.

I'm too young for this! Please, I don't want this!

There was a shuffling sound on the other side of the door, and somewhere in the dark recesses of her mind, she realized that her mother was no longer waiting on the other side.

A baby—I can't have a baby.

The idea was so foreign, so *fucking* bizarre, that despite her sobs, the notion of being pregnant, of having a living, breathing—*was it breathing yet?*—being inside of her was nearly incomprehensible.

And that was all it was: an idea.

A scraping sound, like nails on a chalkboard, brought her back into reality. The girl pulled her forehead away from the door and aggressively wiped the tears away from her eyes with the blade of her hand.

The mixture of emotions roiling inside of her, accelerated by hormonal changes like kerosene fueling flames, came crashing down at once.

And this time, so did her body.

The girl collapsed to the damp floor, her legs crumpling uselessly beneath her.

Her final resting place was just a few inches from the wire coat hanger that her mother had forced through the small opening beneath the door.

"No!" the girl cried.

Not this. This can't be the way.

But despite her pleas, her mother was having none of it.

"Hurry! *He* can't know about this!"

The next word that came out of the girl's mouth was tortured by mucous, rendering it barely intelligible.

"Please!"

But despite the desperation in her voice, Mother was having none of it.

"Hurry!"

* * *

There was blood in the bathtub. Not as much as she would have thought, but enough to tinge the water a pale pink.

The girl was still crying.

"Hush now, we did what was necessary," her mother whispered, her voice oddly detached.

The woman raised the coral sponge and squeezed it on the back of her neck, allowing the water to spill down her back and over her breasts.

The girl watched the water for a moment, her eyes following the lazy rivers of pink fluid as they traced ravines over her naked body.

My blood. I'm being bathed in my blood, she thought briefly, but then instinctively shook her head. *Not my blood—my baby's blood. I'm being bathed in my baby's blood.*

The thought drove a shudder up her spine. Mother took this as a cue to turn her head, and their eyes met.

The girl expected sympathy in the woman's dark green eyes, or at the very least a comforting expression. Instead, she saw neither; her mother's eyes, as well as the rest of her heavily lined face, were a hardened mask that lacked any emotion.

"You did the right thing," her mother informed her, much like a teacher instructing a student that they had come up with the correct answer to a math problem.

'Necessary' had become 'right,' and 'we' had become 'you.' These subtleties were not lost on the girl.

After a short pause, her mother unexpectedly reached out and laid a hand on her cheek. The girl, mistaking this as a comforting gesture, instinctively leaned her head into the cupped hand, wanting—*needing*—some sort of justification, some proof that *she* had indeed done the *right* thing, something beyond her mother's empty words.

But the woman's grip tightened, and the gentle caress became a forceful pinch. The girl in the tub sat up, wincing.

"But you must never forget."

The woman's dark green eyes were focused and unblinking.

"A life for a life, sweets."

Mother paused as silent tears began to pour down the girl's face. When these clear streams eventually met the bathwater, they too took on a tainted pink hue.

Despite her daughter's obvious pain, the woman's grip did not lessen.

"A life for a life. You must never forget."

* * *

The texture beneath the girl's feet slowly transitioned from soft and wet to hard as the ground changed from mud to asphalt.

Head down, she put one foot in front of the other, moving slowly, methodically, traveling in a straight line to nowhere.

One foot, then the next. One foot, and then the next, as dawn slowly began to creep around her.

At some point during her walk, she heard a car approach, only to come to an abrupt stop somewhere off to her right.

Onward she walked.

Then there was a second car, and then a voice.

"Hey! Hey, are you okay?"

Another voice now.

"Look! She's bleeding!"

Something was gently draped over her shoulders—something thick like a blanket, and at long last, her legs stopped moving.

"Call the police! Quick, someone call the police!"

The girl curled into the blanket, her broken mind only barely registering the fact that someone had finally picked up her frail body.

Part I – Sow the Seed

Chapter 1

Arielle Reigns stared the goofy-looking doctor straight in the face.

You think you know everything.

The doctor's smile grew even larger, as if mind-reading were one of the many skills listed on the diplomas wrapped in fancy gold frames and hung around the office.

You think *you know everything, but you don't—you don't know about* this.

Arielle glanced over at her husband for support and was surprised to see that he was staring at her, his light brown eyebrows high on his forehead. He had his typical, *'Well, Arielle?'* expression plastered on his handsome face.

She looked away before anger overcame her, and her gaze fell to her hands tucked in her lap. After a deep breath in through her nose, she looked back at the doctor.

"No," she said bluntly. "I will not undergo any tests."

The smile on the doctor's face slid off like ice warming on a windshield. What replaced it was a look somewhere between concern and frustration.

Dr. Barnes reached up and scratched at the stubble on the back of his head. While some men shaved their heads because they liked the way it looked, or maybe because the style required less work, Dr. Barnes shaved his head because most of it had fallen out naturally. And if nature is guiding you in a direction, why fight it? Why *bother* fighting it?

You can't fight nature.

Just try shooting a hurricane or smothering a tsunami.

"Well," the doctor said at last. The jovial lilt that had been in his voice only moments before had vanished like his smile.

Arielle stared expectantly, but the man just continued to scratch. His long, thin fingers and short nails kept moving up and down the back of his head, making a sound like someone repeatedly doing and then undoing Velcro shoes.

The sound irritated her.

Everything about the man irritated her.

"Well, what?"

Out of the corner of her eye, she saw her husband reach out to her, but she preemptively pulled away, all the while keeping her gaze trained on Dr. Barnes.

"Not now, Martin," she said. Then to the doctor, she continued, "Well, Dr. Barnes, can you help us or not?"

For the second time in less than a minute, the doctor seemed at a loss for words, which annoyed Arielle even further. The man had been all talk five minutes ago, asking personal questions—*How long have you been trying? How are your periods? Regular? Are you having sex when you are ovulating?*—but when she put *him* to the question, the man could only stand there gaping... and scratching his balding fucking head, of course.

"Well?"

Dr. Barnes cleared his throat and brought his hands to his lap. Leaning forward, he finally spoke.

"We need to do some tests first before I—"

Arielle shook her head quickly, her shoulder-length blond hair whipping back and forth. Forced to pull strands away from her face, she wished that she had put it up in a ponytail.

"No," she stated firmly. "No tests."

The doctor turned his dark, beady eyes to Martin.

"No," Arielle interrupted, wagging her finger back and forth in front of her. "No, don't do that. Don't look at him. It's not up to him."

The doctor raised a hand defensively.

"Mrs. Reigns, I didn't mean to—"

"Can you help us or not?"

Dr. Barnes shook his head.

"Without performing tests, there isn't much I can do, I'm afraid. I mean, if you wanted to undergo just a *few* tests, we can consider going the in vitro route."

The man was speaking slowly, and it was obvious to both Arielle and Martin that he was choosing his words very carefully.

"No, not in vitro. It's not natural."

The doctor's expression remained neutral.

"Well, I'm going to be frank with you, Mrs. Reigns, at forty-one years of age—"

"Thirty-nine," Arielle corrected him.

The man stared at her for another moment before interlacing his long fingers and continuing.

"At your age, it's going to be difficult to conceive. I can prescribe some iron pills and something else to try to make sure that you are ovulating. But, without doing some tests—which are completely harmless and minimally invasive—my hands are tied."

"No tests," Arielle reiterated.

Martin reached for her again, and this time she let his hand rest on the back of her arm.

"Sweetie, why don't we get some tests done? I'll have my sperm analyzed and you can—"

She pulled away and turned to face him.

"No tests! I said no tests! What's wrong with you?"

The words had come out more forcefully than she had expected, and Martin recoiled. When his shock faded, it was replaced by a sad and confused look.

He doesn't deserve this.

Arielle took another deep breath in through her nose. She had been scared that something like this might happen, that she would lose her cool.

Her thoughts turned briefly to how well Martin had treated her over the past seven years, ever since the day her maternal instincts had switched on, and from then on out, there had been no way to shut them off.

'It's okay, baby,' Martin had told her countless times. 'You are more than enough for me.'

He would always smirk when he said this, letting her know that he was only partly kidding—joking around to try to lighten the tension… the tension that seemed to constrict around her throat like a noose.

No, Martin definitely didn't deserve her outburst. The doctor, on the other hand…

Arielle was about to apologize to Martin—the words were on the tip of her tongue—when Dr. Barnes suddenly chimed in.

"Mrs. Reigns, if you think you would be more comfortable with a female doctor, I have a colleague—"

Arielle turned back to the doctor, her eyes narrowing.

"What the fuck is wrong with you? I said no tests!"

"Woah!" Martin exclaimed, once again reaching for her.

Arielle stood and her husband's hand fell short. Her blood had started to boil, and she was quickly getting to a point from which even deep breathing wouldn't bring her back.

Dr. Barnes seemed relatively unfazed by her escalating outbursts. In fact, he seemed sympathetic.

"Mrs. Reigns…" His eyes were soft, caring.

For some reason, the doctor's complacency seemed to only infuriate Arielle further. She could even feel beads of sweat forming on her forehead.

It was suddenly hot, *too* hot, in the doctor's small office. It was hot and stifling, and she could feel the walls closing in on her.

Arielle was starting to get tunnel vision.

"I understand what you are going through. I think—"

The doctor's words all melded together, fueling her rage.

Just as she was about to explode, Martin stood and wrapped his arms around her. This time she let him hold her.

You understand nothing, Dr. Barnes! I want a baby and you are a useless fucking tit. Fucking drippy-nosed, goofy-eared, bald fucking quack!

Arielle closed her eyes tightly, trying desperately to control her emotions.

Seven years; for seven years I have been trying to conceive. Seven fucking years.

For the next several moments, all Arielle heard was the sound of blood rushing in her ears and her own heavy breathing.

Calm.

After what felt like minutes, but couldn't possibly have been more than twenty seconds, her anger subsided to a dull throb—it receded just enough to allow embarrassment to creep in.

The doctor is just trying to help, she scolded herself. *Just trying to do his job.*

A moment later, she felt Martin's grip on her shoulders relax.

Calm, Arielle; Dr. Barnes is just trying to help.

The doctor reached up and scratched at the stubble at the back of his head again.

"Just one more question, Mrs. Reigns: have you ever been pregnant before?"

Arielle's eyes snapped open and she lunged at Dr. Barnes, her hands balling into tight fists.

Chapter 2

Neither Martin nor Arielle spoke for the first fifteen minutes of the car ride home. Several times, Martin had cleared his throat as if he intended to say something, but he had refrained. For the most part, this was just fine for Arielle. Staring out the window at the trees as they made their way home was just perfectly fine with her. What wasn't fine, however, was what had happened in the doctor's office.

The next time Martin cleared his throat, whatever had previously held his tongue had disappeared. And what came out of his mouth, somewhat predictably, was a joke. Leave it to Martin to joke at a time like this... at any time, regardless of the situation.

It was one of the many reasons she loved him.

"You know, that's a mean right hook you've got there."

Arielle had been staring at the raw knuckles on her right hand when Martin had started to speak, but now she turned to look at him. When their eyes met, he pulled a hand off of the wheel and pretended to cower against the door.

She couldn't help but smirk.

"Please, Masa, no mo'! I can't take it no mo'!"

Arielle tried her best not to laugh, but she lost the battle. A fountain of giggles came out of her in a spurt.

It wasn't that funny, not really, and it might have even been offensive, but she just couldn't help it. The torrid mix of emotions had bubbled over, and now it was impossible to keep them inside.

After nearly a full minute of laughing, she was left gasping for air with tears streaming down her cheeks.

The next time Martin spoke, his voice was more serious, even if the twinkle in his eye remained.

"Seriously Arielle, that was messed up."

Arielle nodded slowly. Of course, it was messed up.

"We are lucky that Dr. Barnes is such a—"

Arielle turned to him and opened her mouth to say something, to defend herself, but Martin cut her off.

"Let me finish," he urged.

She closed her mouth.

"We are lucky that Dr. Barnes is such a nice guy. Woodward wouldn't have recommended him if he weren't. *And* he helped them conceive Thomas."

Arielle's thoughts turned to their mutual friends, Officer Tony Woodward and his wife, Charlene. And of course, she couldn't help think of their beautiful young boy, Thomas. Thomas, with the golden blond hair and cherub-like cheeks adorned with not two but three dimples.

"I know," Arielle said softly.

She didn't doubt what her husband was saying. And Dr. Barnes seemed like he was actually a nice guy... it was just... just...

"And I'm pretty sure that if it weren't for the fact that both we and Dr. Barnes are friends with the Woodwards, he would be pressing charges by now."

Arielle stared at her husband as he spoke, and despite the condemning nature of his words—this was as aggressive or scolding as the man ever got—she found herself admiring the way he managed to keep his cool even under the most extreme circumstances.

Martin Reigns was undeniably handsome, with a strong jaw adorned with light brown stubble, which was only a shade or two darker than the neatly cropped hair atop his head. There were flecks of gray in the beginnings of his beard and more at his temples. And even though Martin often complained about the gray—*my hair is as white as Charlize Theron's ass*—his hair had just the right amount of it; it had just enough to make him look wiser and not older. Which, in her estimation, not only made him more attractive, but likely helped solidify his spot one of the best real estate brokers in all of South Carolina. A little gray, just enough to show that he had experience, but not enough to suggest that he was too old to compete with the young guns.

"I know it's hard for you, babe."

Martin ran a hand through his hair. It fell back in place, landing exactly the way it had been before. For the hundredth time, Arielle found herself wondering how it did that. With her golden locks, a simple fart in the wind could give her a cowlick for a month.

"I know it's really hard for you, but clearly—*clearly*—blowing up at the doctor is *not* the solution."

Martin made a popping sound with his tongue, reminiscent of the sound her fist had made when it had connected with Dr. Barnes's jaw.

Having completed his speech, Martin finally turned to look at her again. His lips were pressed together with only the corners slightly upturned.

This was as close as Martin got to frowning.

"What do you think?"

Arielle tried not to smile.

I think you are one handsome bastard.

"It *is* hard," she admitted at last. "But I don't want any tests—you know that. I don't... I don't like being prodded, poked, and scraped like some sort of animal before slaughter."

Now it was Martin's turn to laugh, but unlike her giggles, his exclamation was a throaty, bellowing sound that reverberated throughout the cabin.

Arielle frowned.

"No, seriously, Martin. You know how I feel about that."

Martin stopped laughing.

"I've told you before, you're more than enough woman for me."

Arielle felt herself nodding despite herself. For some reason, his words still seemed to soothe her, even though she had heard them many, many times before.

The first time he had said them to her, only about six months after they had started trying, and failing, to conceive, she had been enraged.

'You don't want kids? You don't want to have a child with me?'

But Martin had remained calm during her outburst, and she had soon realized that this was not at all what he'd meant. Martin *did* want a child, she was sure of it. And he wanted one with her. This was just his way of saying, 'If we can't, then *c'est la vie*; I love you, and you are enough to complete me.'

Arielle just wished she could feel the same.

Her eyes drifted back to her throbbing knuckles.

What was *I thinking? Punching a doctor? For what? For suggesting that I take a test? For asking if I had been pregnant before?*

But the answer to that was simple: nothing—she hadn't been thinking at all.

He thinks he knows everything. But he doesn't.

"Imagine we had a girl?"

Arielle's eyes shot up.

"How could one man deal with two women with Floyd Mayweather right hooks?"

Arielle didn't smile, not because she wasn't completely sure who Floyd Mayweather was—she knew enough to get the joke—but because she was immediately preoccupied with the idea of having a girl.

If they had a girl, she would probably have a square jaw like her father, but she would have Arielle's blond hair and green eyes. And hopefully Martin's sense of humor.

"But, seriously, Arielle, why don't we get some tests done? I will stay with you the whole time, and if you feel at all uncomfortable, we can stop immediately."

I feel uncomfortable right now talking about this.

"And I'll get tested too, of course."

Arielle scoffed at this.

"Oh, yeah, easy for you to say. All you have to do is watch some porn and jizz in a cup."

Martin laughed again, this time even louder than before.

"Yeah, they call it Sunday," he added, but Arielle ignored the comment.

"You just jizz in a cup, but I have to be fingered by a stranger. Think about it: a stranger is going to jam his fingers inside me and then use a spoon to scrape my *insides*."

Martin cringed.

"Jesus, Arielle, that's sick."

"Well?"

"Well, let's say you do get pregnant—you are going to have to be inspected then. You know that, right?"

Arielle nodded.

"Sure. But that's different."

"How is that different?" Martin challenged.

Arielle turned her gaze back to the window before answering. As the question hung in the air, Martin pulled up to the long, winding driveway that led to their large stone house. The sun was still high in the sky, and its rays reflected off the many glass windows, creating a sparkling effect. At nearly three thousand square feet and constructed of bleached gray and white stone, their house was beautiful. But with the sun glinting the way that it was? It was surreal—a sparkling beacon signifying home.

She loved their house and she loved Martin.

But it wasn't enough.

Not for her.

"Because then we would be having a child, Martin," she replied as Martin shifted the car into park. "And I've *always* wanted a child."

Chapter 3

With the shades drawn, it was hot in the bedroom; hot *and* humid. It was so hot and humid, in fact, that Arielle felt her forehead break out into a sheen of sweat.

The fact that her heart was racing wasn't helping anything, but that wasn't related to the heat. At least not directly.

"When's the last time we were home at this hour together, babe?"

Arielle ignored her husband and stepped out of the bathroom. Eyes closed, she reached down and grabbed ahold of either side of her t-shirt and forced it downward. It was Martin's t-shirt, an old cotton V-neck that had worn thin, and even when she pushed it down it barely covered her bare ass. A quick shake of her head and her hair fell in front of her face, and she opened her eyes again. Staring through the strands of blond hair, she saw that Martin was still sitting on the side of the bed, magazine in his lap.

He hadn't noticed her yet.

Arielle gently swayed back and forth as she made her way toward the bed, imaginary music playing in her head, the iconic words of 'Lost Together' by Blue Rodeo driving her deeper into the trance.

"Ari—"

Martin swallowed the rest of the word.

Even through the blond hair that still hung in front of her face, Arielle knew that he had finally noticed her. His hands, which had been fiddling with the knot of his tie, froze in midair.

She took another step toward him and pulled the bottom of the t-shirt up slightly, rubbing it back and forth, giving Martin a brief glance of the inside of her thighs.

This was not her, this was someone else; someone had somehow transported themselves into Arielle and turned her into a sexy nymph.

She wasn't entirely sure what had gotten into her. Maybe she felt guilty about the way she had behaved in the doctor's office—*I've been a bad girl*—or maybe she was rewarding Martin for keeping his cool, for putting up with her outbursts.

Maybe she liked it.

Martin *definitely* liked it.

The man swallowed hard and his hands dropped to his sides as Arielle approached, the dangling knot of his tie long forgotten.

"Where's Arielle and what have you done with my wife?" His words came out hoarse, and Arielle had to resist the urge to giggle.

She was within three feet of him now, and she paused to lift her shirt a little higher, revealing more than just her thighs this time.

Martin's breath was coming out in short bursts, and his obvious arousal added to her own. She felt her nipples harden, and when she twisted the shirt again, the fabric rubbed against them and she gasped.

Martin reached for her—nearly lunged at her—but Arielle hopped backward just in time and his arms fell short.

"Lie down," she instructed, her own throat suddenly parched.

A look of confusion crossed Martin's face, so Arielle repeated the order more forcefully.

Martin nodded and obliged.

Arielle's eyes drifted to his khaki slacks.

Now, lying on his back, his arms spread above his head, his arousal was more than palpable—it was plainly obvious.

The tingling that started as sweat on her forehead spread first to her full breasts, then to between her legs. Soon, her entire body was thrumming, their combined sexual energy charging not just the space between them, but their bodies as well.

Arielle pushed her hands downward, driving the t-shirt nearly to her knees. Then, in one smooth motion, she hoisted it completely off her body, revealing herself in all her naked glory. She gave Martin but a second to take it all in before she leaped onto him.

His hands were on her instantly, first clutching at her sides, then grabbing her ass, her breasts, and finally her face as she lowered her head and kissed him.

Arielle felt the hardness of his cock through his pants, and she rubbed her sex up and down it, gliding her body over the whole length of his shaft. Martin nibbled gently at her lower lip, and then his hands were on her hips, driving her onto him.

After only a few seconds of foreplay, neither of them could take it any longer. Arielle reached back, unzipped his pants, and in an instant, Martin slid effortlessly inside her.

Their lovemaking was hungered, fueled by lust and desire, and also by a need.

A need of Arielle to conceive.

When she felt the height of Martin's arousal, she quickly flipped over, pulling him on top of her, driving him deeper inside of her.

"In me," she whispered. "Put a baby in me, Martin."

The man's eyebrows knitted, and he looked shocked by the sudden change of pace, the sudden *businesslike* nature of the act.

He looked shocked and a little hurt.

At first, Arielle feared that she had ruined the moment, but Martin had passed the point of no return. As he grunted into the final climactic moments of ecstasy, Arielle's words echoed in her own head.

Put a baby in me, Martin. Please, please put a baby in me.

* * *

"Where in God's name did that come from?"

Arielle was lying nude on the bed, her knees pulled up to her chin. She had been positioned this way ever since they had finished making love.

She was not so consumed with her need that she was oblivious to the fact that the view she was presently giving Martin was far from flattering.

But it wasn't about him anymore. His role was over.

Now it was up to her, and goddamn it if she wasn't going to use every wives' tale in the book to ensure conception. Even if this meant looking like a pale, shell-less turtle waiting on its back to be picked off by an ostentatious buzzard.

"Martin? Where did you get that?"

Martin rolled a cigar between the thumb and forefinger of his right hand, turning it over to get a better view of the cigar band.

"H. Upmann," he said with an air of pretentiousness. "Magnum Fifty. From Cuba."

Arielle rolled her eyes.

"I meant who gave it to you?"

Martin snipped the end off the cigar and brought it to his lips.

"A client."

When she just stared, he continued.

"Sold the business complex on Park Ave. Got a fat commission check." He pulled the cigar from his lips and stared at it. "And a fat cigar."

Arielle gave him a moment to enjoy his cigar, but when he brought the lighter to within a few inches of it, she spoke up.

"You aren't going to light that in here."

Martin raised an eyebrow, his eyes twinkling mischievously. "No?"

He brought the lighter closer, teasing her. The end of the cigar started to darken.

"And what are you going to do about it, Mrs. Kegel?"

She attempted to swat the lighter away, but she missed and nearly rolled over. Her hands shot out and she quickly grabbed her knees again.

Martin chuckled and leaned away from her. He brought the lighter to the end of the cigar.

"Martin!" she shouted.

"Just this once," he said. "Because when we have the baby, I will have to stop smoking altogether."

Arielle shook her head and tried to scold him, but a smile found its way on her full lips instead. He knew just what to say to get his way.

Martin didn't wait for a response before proceeding to light the end of the cigar.

It was clear by the expression on his face that he knew he had won. Her smile told him so.

And she was helpless to conceal it.

"Just this once," she affirmed, squeezing her knees close to her chest and holding her breath.

Just this once... because after this I will be pregnant.

Chapter 4

"Saint Raymond Nonnatus," Arielle whispered.

She clicked the mouse, and her face was immediately bathed in the frosty blue glow from her computer screen.

The painting on-screen depicted a man with short brown hair and an impossibly thick beard that hung nearly to the hollow of his throat. He was wearing a strange red shawl that covered his shoulders, and a white flowing gown that flooded to his ankles where it gave way to clichéd brown strap sandals. Grasped in his right hand and held out in front of him was what looked like a golden cup. The man held something else in his other hand—a scepter? A fancy mirror?—which was aimed high in the sky like some sort of beacon.

For all Arielle knew, it *was* a beacon, a signal to the heavens. *Giveth this woman a babe.*

"Nonnatus," she repeated, enjoying the way the name rolled off her tongue. "Nonnnn—"

A hand rested on her shoulder, and she nearly jumped out of her skin.

"Jesus!" she swore, turning to face Martin.

There was a goofy look on his face, one that made him look far younger than his forty-odd years. He looked like a little boy, and the fact that he was holding a bowl of cereal in one hand only perpetuated this image. His brown eyes squinted as he hovered over her, staring intently at her computer screen.

"Yeah, it could be him," he affirmed, nodding. He leaned away and brought another spoonful of cereal to his mouth. "Sure looks like Jesus."

Arielle shook her head.

"No, it's not Jesus. It's Saint—" She glanced back at the screen. "—Saint Raymond Nonnatus. The patron saint of conception."

She felt Martin lean over her again, but this time he stretched so far that she was essentially giving him a piggyback. The sweet smell of Fruitee-O's or whatever cereal he was eating mixed with the equally saccharine scent of milk filled her nostrils.

How can he eat that stuff?

"Hmm… looks like the patron saint of cross-dressing to me."

He pulled back and Arielle suppressed a smile.

Martin had a point.

"But look." She switched to another browser window. A bulletin board popped onto the screen. "There are hundreds, if not thousands, of people that swear by this guy. These women, they—"

"—are desperate and lonely?" Martin offered.

Arielle ignored him.

"They went once, just once, and prayed to this—"

"—crossdressing makeup artist—"

"—Saint, and they conceived shortly thereafter."

Martin's expression changed from mocking to one of incredulity. He stared at her for a moment, as if sizing her up. Arielle refused to back down and stared back.

He brought another spoonful of cereal to his mouth.

"You're serious?"

Arielle nodded.

Chew, chew, chew.

"Serious, serious? Like you're going to do this, serious?"

Her gaze faltered, but only for a moment.

She clasped her hands together and lay them on her lap.

"I'm willing to try anything at this point."

Martin continued to stare, unabashedly sizing her up now. "Nana-tits?"

"Nonnatus."

Martin made a 'What the fuck?' face and turned and went to the sink. She heard him sigh before dropping his empty bowl into the metal basin. There was an awkward moment where she just stared at his back, his hands clutching the sides of the sink, his head hung low. But when he turned back to face her, his expression was unexpectedly neutral.

"Look, Air, I'm all for having sex on a schedule like a union worker, and I even don't mind your 'orchid trying to hold onto dew' pose after sex. But, but this—" He gestured toward her computer screen. "—this *Nana-tits* is too much."

Arielle could feel her face begin to tingle. She was pretty sure that the color of her cheeks matched the crimson color of Saint Nonnatus's robes.

Anger crept in behind the embarrassment.

"Arielle, did you ever think that it's just not meant to be? That maybe we can be happy without children? Or—God forbid—adopt a child?"

Arielle's face transitioned from crimson to purple. She jumped to her feet so quickly that the computer chair rolled all the way to the far wall.

In all seven years of trying to conceive, this was the first time he had ever said anything like this. And he chose now, wearing a crappy cotton t-shirt and plaid pajama bottoms with milk clinging to just beneath his bottom lip, to say it.

Arielle lost it.

"Without children? *Without children?* Martin, what the fuck are you saying? Don't you want to have kids with me?"

Martin recoiled as if he had been struck, and his face got all screwed up. It looked like he was having a stroke.

"I—I—"

"You really don't want to have kids?"

The last thing Arielle wanted to do was cry, but she was helpless to control the tears that welled from somewhere inside her lids. This tsunami of emotions was extreme even for her. But this was what her life had become lately; just a light breeze pushing her hair out of perfect and Arielle wouldn't know if she would cry, scream, or pass out.

This time, however, it seemed like it was time to cry.

Martin recovered from the initial shock of her tantrum and quickly made his way over to her, wrapping his burly arms protectively around her.

"Of course I want to have kids, Air, you know that."

Arielle sniffed and nodded. She buried her head in his t-shirt, enjoying the way it smelled faintly of vanilla.

They stayed in that pose for a moment or two without speaking. She knew she should say something, that she should apologize, but she couldn't; she was too busy holding back more tears like the Hoover Dam.

"Hey, Arielle?" Martin said at last. He gestured to the computer screen with his chin. "Do you think Nana-tits is gonna breastfeed when we finally have our baby?"

Arielle laughed. She couldn't help it. Martin had a way of doing that; getting her to laugh even during the most stressful and anxiety-ridden situations.

Even when laughing was the last thing in the world she wanted to do.

Chapter 5

Of course, Martin went with her.

Despite everything that he said—which ranged from mocking, to incredulous, to dumbfounded—he eventually agreed to get in the car and drive her to the church.

Just as Arielle had known he would.

Now, standing at the base of a large, bleached staircase, staring up at the ornate church, Arielle felt silly. And with the sun beating down on her, causing sweat to drip down her back before being soaked up by her pale blue sundress, she felt incredibly uncomfortable as well.

For what it was worth, Martin looked worse. She couldn't tell if it was the heat, the church, or the fact that he seemed to have put on a few extra pounds ever since he had left his real estate firm to go out on his own. But whatever it was that was irking him this day, it was clearly etched on his handsome face: his eyebrows were knitted, giving him unsightly creases at the top of his nose, and the corners of his mouth, so very often leaning upward in a grin or the beginnings of a smile, were downturned. And he, like Arielle, was covered with a thin layer of sweat.

What the hell are we doing here?

The front of the church was adorned with several massive stained glass windows. Two huge Corinthian pillars held up a peaked awning that overhung a ridiculously large wooden door.

It was a Catholic church, which made sense to Arielle. After all, not only was this the home of Saint Raymond Nonnatus, but she *was* Catholic. Not Catholic in a churchgoing, God-fearing way, but in the way a person is Jewish despite chowing down on bacon cheeseburgers on the weekend. She was a Catholic *now*, because she needed to be Catholic—it suited her purpose.

And right now she needed Saint Nonnatus.

Arielle turned to face her husband, who was staring up at the church like a layman charged with writing a dissertation on a Jackson Pollock painting.

"You ready?"

Martin's answer was immediate and unambiguous.

"No."

He opened his mouth to add something else, but decided better of it. It didn't matter; Arielle knew what he wanted to say. She knew because the same words were bouncing around in her blond skull.

What are we doing here?

"It will be quick... let's get it over with. Besides," she said, gesturing toward the awning and the large wooden door, "I need to get into the shade."

Martin nodded and hooked arms with her.

"Let's do this," he grumbled, and together they made their way up the church steps.

Arielle didn't think it was possible, but she felt more uncomfortable *inside* the church than she had been staring at the facade.

The cool church interior was predictably gloomy, with light only coming from two sources: weak streaks of colored rays of sun that squeezed through thick panes of stained glass, and a series of candles that seemed to be scattered about the church. Like forgotten relics, the candles dripped waxed everywhere: on makeshift altars, on the handles of massive brass candle holders, and even on what looked like a tapestry-covered coffin.

And then there was the smell: the inside of the church smelled like a noxious concoction of bitter incense and must.

Arielle crinkled her nose.

As she waited for her eyes to adjust to the dramatic change in light, she began inspecting the church's other patrons. There were only a handful of people in the church, mostly women, which was odd for a Sunday afternoon—or so she thought.

Isn't Sunday their busy day?

As it was, most of the other churchgoers seemed caught up in their business, and as strange and out of place as Arielle felt entering the church, they took no notice of either her or Martin.

There was an elderly woman with long, frizzy hair kneeling on a pew, her hands clasped together so tightly that Arielle thought she might crush the plastic rosary that was intertwined between her fingers.

Another woman was weeping silently over a table of candles, a thin wooden stick with the end alight in her trembling hand, casting flickering shadows across her hawkish features.

A third woman stood in the center of the room, her head high, her eyes tightly closed. Her hands hung at her sides, palms out, as if she expected the rays of colored light in which she stood would suddenly beam her up and out of the church… and maybe off this earth.

What are we doing here? Arielle wondered for what felt like the hundredth time. *What are we doing in this place of death and mourning? Of sadness? We are not like this.*

She turned to stare at Martin.

He looked constipated. Or maybe like he was having a stroke.

We are usually *not like this.*

"What do we do now?" Martin asked out of the corner of his mouth.

When he turned to face her, he clearly didn't expect her to be staring at him. His eyes bulged.

"What?"

Arielle shook her head.

"Nothing."

Martin tapped the toe of his light gray loafer.

"Well, what do we do now, Mother Teresa?"

Arielle went back to scanning the inside of the church. She didn't bother answering her husband, deciding instead that her efforts were best spent searching for divine inspiration.

The truth was, she had no idea what to do next. She couldn't remember the last time she had been in church, but assumed it had been when she still crapped her pants.

"Air? What—?"

Arielle shushed him.

Her eyes gradually made their way back to the woman hovering over the table with all the candles. She was pretty sure that this was where you lit candles for the dead—the exact opposite reason why they were here—but for some reason, she was drawn to that spot.

"Come on," she grumbled, giving Martin's arm a tug.

The table of candles was pressed against the side wall, and Arielle dragged Martin over to it. The woman with the shaking hands had since lit her candle and now hovered over it, humming, her back to them.

When Arielle was just a few feet from the table, she noticed it: a figure wearing red-and-white robes, just like she had seen on the Internet. It was a painting of Saint Raymond Nonnatus in a tacky gold frame leaning up against the wall. Just in front of the picture was a dark ceramic bowl, inside of which were a handful of small turquoise stones.

"There," she whispered, extending a finger toward the painting, trying her best not to disturb the mourning woman.

Martin nodded, but the confused look on his face remained.

"I think we take a—"

The woman hovering over the candles turned to face Arielle.

She was younger than Arielle might have expected based on her pointy features. Her smooth face was covered in strands of jet-black hair that were nearly indistinguishable from the streaks of teary mascara that marked her cheeks.

"Please, my—"

The woman had begun saying something as she turned, but when her eyes met Arielle's, her expression immediately changed. The woman's dark eyebrows furrowed, her eyes somehow became beady, and something akin to recognition crossed her face.

"*Filius obcisor*," the woman hissed.

Arielle cringed and shrunk away from her.

What the fuck?

Martin, who didn't appear to have even noticed the weeping woman, reached into the bowl of turquoise stones.

"Air, I think you put one of these in if…" He pulled out one of the stones and rubbed it between his fingers. It was smooth, like marble.

The woman with the black hair turned to Martin, and Arielle took another step backward. Her heart raced. She could feel all of the muscles in her face go slack, as if the anger and hatred in the strange woman's eyes had somehow taxed her ability to form an expression.

Inside, her mind was twisting into a carnival pretzel.

"You already took one out," she spat.

Martin finally acknowledged the woman. Whatever hold the woman had on Arielle apparently did not extend to him.

"Huh?" Martin held the stone up so that it caught a ray of stained glass sunlight. "This? It's just a—"

"You already took one out!" the woman hissed. "You are supposed to put one in."

Martin made a face as he tossed the stone back into the bowl, where it landed with a loud clack.

"It's just a rock," he finished with a shrug.

The woman turned back to Arielle.

"*Filius obcisor*! You took one out, you don't get to put one back in! *Filius obcisor*!"

"I put it back," Martin informed her, but his comment went ignored. "Didn't you see?"

Arielle felt like crying.

"*Filius obcisor*! You took one out!"

Who is this fucking psycho and what is she saying?

Martin stepped between them.

"Woah, now. I don't know—"

"A LIFE FOR A LIFE!" the woman suddenly screamed.

The tears that had been welling behind Arielle's eyes suddenly evaporated and were immediately replaced by fury.

She stepped past Martin and grabbed the woman by the arm.

"What the *fuck* did you say?"

Spit dribbled from Arielle's lip, but she refused to wipe it away. She squeezed the woman's triceps so hard that her fingers started to ache.

"What did you say?"

The woman failed to acknowledge either Arielle's words or her grasp. Instead, her expression twisted into a sneer. Her face, which before might have before been described as cute if pointy, was suddenly all angles and shadows; hideous.

"*Filius obcisor.*" The woman's voice was barely a whisper now.

"No, not that. What *else* did you say?"

The shock that had gripped Martin suddenly thawed. Apparently realizing that the bizarre situation was about to reach a head, he leaned over and tried to separate the two women. It took him three tries to pry Arielle's fingers from the woman's arm.

"Let go, Arielle," he grumbled.

Arielle ignored him.

"What did you say?" she repeated between gritted teeth.

None of the malice she laced her words with seemed to matter; the stupid fucking words—*Filius obcisor*—that the woman uttered were some sort of anti-venom.

"Arielle, let's get out of here."

Martin tried to turn her, but Arielle held her ground.

Did she really say what I think she did?

She couldn't let it go... the only person who had ever said that to her had been—

"*Filius obcisor!*"

"What did you say to me, you fucking bitch?"

"Woah! Arielle, calm down. Let's just get out of here."

She felt Martin's hands grab her by the shoulders and attempt to guide her toward the door. This time she let him; if she didn't, she knew that Martin would eventually just pick her up and haul her out of there, whether she wanted to leave or not.

"*Filius obcisor!*"

The strange words sounded as if they were coming at her in stereo now, and Arielle managed with great effort to tear her eyes from the psycho with the black hair. The other two women that had been in the church when they had arrived were now staring at her, their own lips twisted in matching sneers.

"*Filius obcisor!*" all three women shouted in unison.

What the fuck?

Arielle didn't know if she said the words, if Martin had, or if she just thought them.

But they had never been more appropriate.

What the FUCK?!

The woman in the pews stepped into the aisle and her rosary, clutched so desperately only moments earlier, fell to the ground in a clatter, unwanted, useless.

"*Filius obcisor!*" she hissed.

The third woman was still standing in the glow of the stained glass, but now her head was facing forward and her eyes were not trained on Martin, who had succeeded in getting them both within a few feet of the large wooden door, but on her.

In her.

"*Filius obcisor! Filius obcisor! Filius obcisor!!!*"

To continue reading, grab your copy of [MOTHER](#) today!

Sign up for my no-spam newsletter and be the first to know about new releases, sales and exclusive contests!

Just go to *www.PTLBooks.com.*

You can also keep up to date by 'liking' my Facebook page @authorpatricklogan

And don't forget to grab your copy of MOTHER, Book 1 of the *Family Value Trilogy.*
Available now!

Made in United States
North Haven, CT
21 January 2025

64743199R00098